That Other Egypt

by

Rhys Hughes

That Other Egypt
by Rhys Hughes

ISBN: 978-1-913766-37-5

Publication Date: 2025

Contents

This book is
dedicated to my wife
Maithreyi

Mummyfixation

First they found the mummy of the daddy. Then they found the mummies of the brothers and sisters, uncles and aunts. Finally they found mummies of the little ones, the brats and sprats.

They never found the mummy of the mummy, because her little ones had already had brats and sprats of their own, changing the mummy into a grandmummy, also called a *sarcophagus gran*, which isn't like a mummy at all, being distinctly more shrivelled.

In fact the brats and sprats of the little ones had also had little ones at some point, further transmuting the mummy into a great-grandmummy, a thing so withered, delicate and crispy that it crunches and crackles like an autumn leaf when a shadow falls on it.

It gets worse if the brats and sprats of the brats and sprats have brats and sprats of their own, and so on. Mini-mummies, micro-mummies and nano-mummies are already of increasingly limited use to archaeologists, but pico-mummies, femto-mummies and atto-mummies hardly exist and in electron microscopes remain specks.

Nobody at all loves those mummies. And an unloved mummy is very dangerous. An unloved mummy will get up on the most desiccated legs to lurch over and slap a daddy hard. That's why, by law, archaeologists who explore tombs are always unmarried childless men. But things can still go wrong even when precautions are taken.

These most unloved, thus most hazardous, mummies are invisible to the naked eye, but they can deliver a slap that is fatal to a human being by entering the bloodstream and going on a rampage like a virus, converting healthy cells into miniscule mummies also, until what was once a grown professional becomes a Pharaonic husk.

To protect themselves, the tomb raiders wear suits and masks on the slight chance they are daddies without knowing it. After all, they went to universities when they were younger, and students throw parties, and we all know what can happen where there is wine, music, dancing. It pays to be extra safe, to make that special effort.

In this particular tomb there was something wrong in the arrangement of the coffins and the precious objects stacked all around them, but it was difficult to say exactly *what* the problem was. It wasn't quite sinister, but certainly Carter felt uneasy for a reason.

"Anyone else got the heebies or jeebies today?"

Through the thick mask his voice was distorted and seemed to come from somewhere else, from the unlighted corners of the room, from the lips of the painted figures on the walls, or perhaps from the grotesquely twisted and mocking mouths of the mummies themselves. Glances were exchanged through crystalline goggles.

"I've got a few of the latter," confessed Carter.

They all had the same name, a custom that made accountability more difficult but which facilitated a positive solidarity in the face of criticisms of the ethics of the profession. Carter nodded and said, "Thanks for being honest." Then he turned to the others. "There is no shame in admitting to a little fear now and then, trust me."

"I had a heeby earlier, maybe one and a half."

"Who said that?"

"I did, sir. Me over here."

"Ah, Carter! One and a half, eh? Well, we can round that up to two. I am willing to state that *right now* there are six or seven heebies inside me, and four very definite jeebies. That doesn't bode too well, I would say. It seems to me that we should work fast and try to get out of here as soon as possible. I loathe inexplicable anxieties!"

"I've got an idea, sir."

"Have you Carter? Please share it," said Carter.

"Might it simply be," responded Carter slowly, "that the unique shape of this pyramid has unsettled us?"

"Go on, Carter," urged Carter, frowning.

"I mean it's the first *inverted* pyramid we've entered or even seen and perhaps subconsciously our minds can't cope with that fact, so they detect heebies and jeebies where there aren't any. I don't desire to make light of the situation but that's my explanation."

"A clever argument," said a thoughtful Carter.

Carter beamed at this praise.

"And a plausible one too," added Carter.

They were reassured, or rather they told themselves that they ought to be reassured, and they proceeded to act as if they really were, penetrating still deeper into the sequence of tombs, each of which was separated by a secret door from the preceding one. To locate these doors and open them with minimal damage was part of an archaeologist's training. Carter was especially good at picking ancient locks.

The other Carters were in awe of him for this, but in truth they were also in awe of each other for other reasons. Every Carter in awe of every other Carter, such was the achieved ideal.

Carter had gone ahead into the gloom, the beam of his electric torch lancing air that had been undisturbed for millennia, and now he stood in the final tomb, the chamber furthest from the entrance they had forced in the wall of the pyramid. He cleared his throat loudly to rivet attention, for the plates of focus are held together by such throat rivets to form the hulls of the ships of archaeological science.

"I have bad news, sir."

"What is it, Carter?" demanded Carter.

"I've just removed the lid of a curiously warped coffin and looked at the contents and they aren't normal."

"Speak plainly, Carter," insisted Carter.

"Truly there *are* heebies and jeebies here but… I'm not sure how to break it gently… all are mummified!"

There was silence as they digested this information.

"Is that possible?" cried Carter.

"Come and see for yourself," replied Carter.

All the Carters filed through the little doorway into the last tomb and took it in turns to peer into the coffin that rested in the exact centre of the chamber. Several dozen heebies and an equal number of jeebies had been placed in there side by side and they were mummies, no doubt about it. A baffled and disturbed Carter reached out a gloved finger to poke one. Yes, it was real. This was no hallucination.

"What can it mean, sir?"

Carter clutched the edge of the coffin to steady himself.

"It's finally happened!"

"What has finally happened, sir?"

"We took a wrong turning."

The Carters looked at each other again and they widened their eyes, for this was something else they were very good at, eye widening, and at university they had passed exams in the subject. Mouth gaping too; but in a mask a mouth is like a fish in night water, slippery and hard to catch or even feed. So eyes took priority in the calculus of astonishment, goggles magnifying them like insolent mirrors.

"Are you referring to Aegypt?" asked Carter.

"Where else?" cried Carter.

"The chances of accidentally entering—"

Carter sighed, disturbing the dead air like the flapping of the wings of a political party with schismatic tendencies. "I know, I know, the chances are even lower than entering a time warp, a hotel recycled from the glove of a giant or the elegant woman in a maroon hat you see sauntering down the street one day. Select your own implausible comparison! Nonetheless, what's the alternative explanation?"

"Aegypt, not Egypt," whistled the Carters superstitiously.

Carter nodded, then grunted.

"Nice grunting," said Carter, who was musical.

The other Carters concurred.

"Thanks," acknowledged Carter, "but I have a bad feeling about this. I know we're meant to have bad feelings while working, it's part of what we do, but bad feelings are like cheeses, some smell better or worse than others, and this one pongs like the most powerful gorgonzola. If we are really in Aegypt, rather than Egypt, how will we get out again? We'll be stuck here for the rest of our lives; and too many aspects are different in this land for us to ever truly adjust."

The Carter who had found the mummified heebies and jeebies rubbed his jaw. "Just because we encountered something impossible in our world doesn't mean we are in another. It could simply be that no one ever found any heeby or jeeby mummies until now. Heebies and jeebies only exist in the mind, yes? They are purely psychological states, and no more. But we don't know how old this pyramid is."

"You're suggesting that in the distant past maybe heebies and jeebies occupied an external environment and that they migrated into our heads since this tomb was sealed millennia ago? I guess that's possible. I hope it's true. If we find more anomalies—"

"Yes! They were plausible fauna once!" Carter desperately wanted to cling to any hope, but Carter retorted:

"No fossil of a heeby or jeeby has ever been discovered. I know that fossilisation is a matter of extraordinary circumstance and that millions of species undoubtedly existed of which there's no fossil record, but I'm still inclined to believe that heebies and jeebies never had more than a mental reality in our world, thus these mummies indicate that we are in a parallel dimension right now, trapped forever."

Carter shrugged and turned to retrace his steps.

"I don't feel safe in an inverted pyramid, especially one that might be located deep inside Aegypt. Let's go."

He led them back along the tortuous route to the entrance hole. Bright daylight made them squint their qualified eyes as they crawled one by one through the ragged gap. They stretched in the sun. Not in the sun exactly, for that would have vaporised them in a millisecond, but in the metaphor. They basked and gazed around, as so many gazers have done throughout human and non-human history, and wondered if this was their new home for the remainder of their lives. If so, would it contain nice surprises and kind words, soft seats, fresh linen, bagels?

They could only hope so. They couldn't pray, because none of them was religious. Hope was all they had. Without being given permission, they divested themselves of their suits and masks and Carter didn't stop them. In fact he did exactly the same thing.

Aegypt was a fabled place that just happened to be true. It had always existed probably, but who knew for sure? Crossing the border into Aegypt entailed passing through an invisible band that was as narrow as two short strides. All travellers felt nothing; but the few who suddenly stopped, for whatever reason, inside the band, turned at right angles and walked down the corridor it formed, would find it became wider, opened out gradually, disgorged itself and them into a country with only surface resemblances to the familiar Egypt they were expecting.

This new land was Aegypt and was part of an alternative Earth and it was extremely difficult to find one's way back out of it. One would have to locate and enter another invisible band and use it as a corridor going in the opposite direction, but these bands were not only invisible, they were undetectable by all known scientific apparatus, even devices designed by the greatest boffins, those who were bald.

And the bands fluctuated and wandered, making it impossible to map them. Discovery was only by accident. Carter had no need to explain this to the Carters under him. They had read as part of their training, *Carters' Cryptic Aegypt Tips* by Carter and Carter.

Carter said, "We might as well head towards the city."

"Which one?" frowned Carter.

"The equivalent of Cairo, I believe it's called Qairo. We can explain our situation and hope for understanding from the authorities. We surely can't be the first to stray across the worlds. I bet there are individuals on our Earth who originally came from here."

"I am certain you're right, Carter. These things happen. Lost people from both dimensions probably equal out numerically and qualitatively. No need for pessimism at this stage."

Carter took a compass reading. "Qairo is that way."

They set off. They tramped.

After an hour Carter asked, "By which stage will there be some need for pessimism, sir?" He was squinting.

"I'll be sure to inform you," snarled Carter, sweating.

"Please don't forget, sir!"

They all squinted or sweated now, some saving time by doing both at once; and the inverted pyramid retreated into the distance, became a blur, while other inverted pyramids, having appeared like shimmering smudges on the horizon ahead, gradually took firmer form. Carter, more observant than his companions, noticed and said, "Funny how they take firmer form while the muscles of my legs soften."

"All of us are ripening fast," remarked Carter.

The others nodded, but not in solidarity, because little about the way they acted and felt was solid now; but they kept going. The sand sapped their energy but protected their ankles from injury. Every advantage has a hidden disadvantage, and vice versa, isn't this so? The blood pounded in their ears or perhaps it was the throb of distant drums or maybe… yes the sound actually belonged to hoofed legs.

A robed rider on a camel was catching them up.

Carter turned in confrontation.

"Remember, men, that he could be hostile or friendly, or even both at the same time. He might want to give us dates or ask us out on them. He possibly hopes to sell us into slavery or buy our silence. Maybe he wishes to compare and contrast us to baboons."

"How shall we cope, sir?"

"Be tolerant. Any of us would be capable of doing any of those things too, if our roles were reversed. Come to think of it, it's feasible he wants us to reverse roles, but be warned that if you reverse a role the filling falls out. I learned this at university."

"So did we," chorused the Carters hoarsely.

"Leave the talking to me."

"Salaam my friends! How do you do?"

The stranger was affable and utterly muffled in the striped fabric of his robes. Affable and muffled is a fine combination at certain times, they knew. Carter raised an arm in salute.

"We are doing reasonably well, but we could be doing better. We are neither wholly in crisis nor in clover."

"You are new to this world? I can see by your stances that Aegypt is not your native land. You are lost."

The camel was immense and had eyes that were sad but humorous, as if it had recently finished reading an ironically bittersweet novel, but that was unlikely, for the fiction published in desert regions tends to be sober and utilitarian even when it is wondrous and escapist. The rider atop the beast displayed only his own eyes.

"We are archaeologists," declared Carter.

"Of course you are! Very few people of other professions ever cross over between the worlds. That is probably why I have never managed to find the passage that leads to yours."

Carter took the bait. "What is it that you do?"

"I follow an ancient trade!"

The figure made a cryptic cutting motion with his hands followed by a plucking gesture and then acted as if he were wrapping an invisible gift for a close friend he had fallen out with.

No Carter understood any of this. They were men, certainly, but none of them were true geniuses. Which raises the question, why don't women pick this career? For reasons unknown, no women apply for the position. None are persuaded, despite financial inducements and proffered bonuses of other kinds. They aren't interested.

"Why, my naïve friends! I am a mummifier!"

"You?" croaked Carter.

"The job still exists?" blurted Carter.

"Yes, I make mummies. I make new ones every day. I've made more mummies in my career than there are grains of sand in this desert. No one is more industrious at this art than am I."

"But the art of making mummies is obsolete," cried Carter, "and has been for centuries. It belongs to a younger world, to an infantile period of history, to the toddler eras of humanity."

The enigmatic eyes glinted. "True in *your* world. But in Aegypt there was no cessation of mummification. We kept at it and progressed beyond your capabilities. I have mummified things you would deem ineligible for the honour. Not just daddies, sons, daughters, cousins and other relatives, but the environment itself, abstract concepts, blinks, doubts, hugs, songs, riddles, rumours, clouds, seas, the very sneeze of a nose. I've mummified the inner angles of rainbows and smiles."

Carter snorted. "How can one mummify a sea?"

"By removing the moisture and replacing it with stuffing. How else? You strike me as sadly conservative."

"I just don't believe you. Prove it!" snapped Carter.

The mummifier bowed his head.

"This camel is a mummy, for instance. Behold!"

And with a little knife that he drew from some hidden fold of his robe he made an incision in the hump and drew out a wad of cotton. The beast grinned at this, as if it tickled. Then the man held up the knife to flash and scintillate in the sunlight. "The knife is also a mummy… and so is the sun that shines upon it… I mummified them!"

"Preposterous," said Carter.

But the mummifier hurled the knife into the sky with immense force. His aim was good and the spinning blade struck the centre of the blinding ball of molten hydrogen and stuck there, handle quivering with a musical note as streams of stuffing dribbled down the face of the star. The Carters no longer could seek refuge in disbelief.

Finally Carter muttered, "What *isn't* a mummy here?"

"Nothing," came the reply.

"Nothing at all?"

"Almost nothing. One thing remains."

"Is it the world itself?"

"No. I long ago opened that up, extracted the magma and replaced it with a selection of variegated cushions and an enormously soft pillow for the core. The same is true of the other planets. Every star in the sky, every quasar, every dream and desire, every number, even zero and infinity, are mummies. I have been very busy."

"So what is next?"

"Time is the last thing remaining to be mummified. Time itself. And despite your sceptical facial expressions, I know you are familiar with it, for it frames all you do. Usually called t in equations, it stops everything from happening at once while ensuring that it does happen. It is a tyrant and a comfort, a dawdle and a race."

"Time is an arrow," said Carter mournfully.

"So I've heard. But no matter how sharp are its barbs I will mummify it successfully. I've mummified many edges and points in my career, all of them in fact. The time has come to finish the job and make time into a mummy. You have arrived in Aegypt at a significant moment. This will be something to remember. Watch!"

Carter croaked, "If you mummify time, won't time stop? We will be suspended eternally in one moment!"

The mummifier ignored him and Carter acted.

He lunged forward to pull the fellow off the camel but was too feeble to achieve his aim. The mummified heat of the wounded sun had drained him of energy. He yanked ineffectually at the robes while the mummifier shook him off and reached out to tear the fabric of time with bare hands, opening a rent in the concept of duration.

Carter gazed into the expanding hole despite his better judgment. He saw unborn moments, shaped like potentials but soft and flexible, then he turned away his head and shut tight his eyes, too squeamish to face these embryos of the future. Yet he was aware that the mummifier was stuffing the space beyond the gap with padding…

Then the padding was exhausted and instead…

Something touched his arm. He opened his eyes, blinked at the owner of the fingers that were caressing him. A waiter came to their table with a tray and poured coffee into little cups. The exotic sounds of Qairo washed over them. Carter lifted his drink slowly and tried to concentrate on what was being said to him while he sipped.

"Your assumption was wrong. Mummification of time won't suspend time. When pharaohs are turned into mummies, it doesn't fix them in the identities they formerly possessed. By no means! They don't remain the pharaohs they were. They don't remain people at all. Their bodies don't decay in the normal way, true, but only at the price of a serious withering and mangling; and in this radical new form they wait patiently to meet the archaeologists who will unearth them."

"Is this coffee a mummy?"

"Of course! And so is the waiter who brought it. Please pay attention, Carter, and when the explanation is over we can enjoy our date properly. Time is like that pharaoh. It has been preserved from regular decay, saved from passing in the typical fashion, but history has been horribly distorted as a result. The process of mummifying time has disfigured both the past and present. That doesn't matter. The essential point is that my mission is finished. I have mummified everything."

"Is love a mummy too?"

"My darling, even *nothingness* is a mummy now. But let's change the subject. I must express how thrilled I am that you agreed to come out on a romantic date with me. Of all the Carters, you're the only one who caught my eye. I mean it. The others just aren't my type. Are they truly as dull as they seem? I think they assumed I was a man beneath my robes. How did you work out I was a woman?"

Carter put down his cup in surprise. "You are?"

"Didn't you suspect?"

"I'm an archaeologist. I barely know what a woman is. I thought your high voice and curvaceous figure were due to cotton balls and other kinds of padding, that self-mummification was responsible for the sway of your hips, fullness of your lips, the allure of the mystery of your enigma. Yes, I did go to university and yes, students do throw parties, and yes, there was wine, music and dancing, but that was only in *theory* and never applied. I took for granted you were a man."

"But now? Isn't the maroon hat a clue?"

"It should be, I guess. I'm sorry. I have much to learn. Let's go for a stroll by the river this evening."

"Under the mummified moon? How sensuous."

"Yes, full and bandaged…"

"That's when its mummified light is most like mummified butter that can be spread on our togetherness."

"There's just one thing that bothers me…" Carter found it difficult to gaze directly into her eyes. "When you were stuffing time and ran out of pillows, did you really have to use all the other Carters instead? I can still hear them kicking feebly and squealing in every second of every minute that passes and it's very distracting."

"Don't worry, dearest, it's unlikely they will ever break out. I sewed up the rent in time with my strongest thread. And they are too timid to try now anyway. They have lost all their courage. When they worked for you they were brave. But no longer."

"Why the change?" wondered Carter.

"I mummified you too, when you weren't looking. You are a mummy through and through. It was for the best. You're in my world now and it's important that you fit in, my darling."

"How does that make the Carters less brave?"

She took his hand, her clever fingers rustling like shed snake skins as they entwined with his, and said, "Technically they still work for you. So they are mummy's boys. It is as simple and logical as that. Shall we lean across the table and kiss passionately, knocking over the cups, spilling the cooling wrinkled mummified coffee?"

Carter agreed. It was time.

Nile by Mouth

It was certainly a surprise to Beaumont and an even bigger one to his wife when his head began to change shape. At first a lump appeared on the top of his skull and he wondered if he might have banged his head without being aware of it, perhaps on the headboard of the bed during a troubled sleep, but the swelling didn't go down.

"Your cheekbones are altering too," Francine said.

"Maybe I have a disease."

"Something that distorts your bones?"

"There are plenty of conditions that can do that, not all of them due to bacteria or viruses. I guess I ought to go and see the doctor. I will arrange an appointment for next week."

"In the meantime, here is your breakfast."

"What about you?"

"I have to go to the salon."

"Changing your hairstyle again, are you?"

"Better than changing the shape of my head, darling, as I'm sure you will agree. Take care and see you later."

Beaumont waved his spoon.

Francine left the house and he was left alone and as he stirred yoghurt into his muesli he had the bizarre impression that the flakes of oats, nuts and dried fruits were tiny workers on an immense project, all prone in the bowl like that, sleeping after a hard day's toil. But before he could focus his attention on them fully, they were already blended with the yoghurt, a deluge of creaminess that abruptly ended the vision, as if the little men in the bowl had been covered by one enormous white quilt that had burst to scatter its fluffy cotton innards everywhere.

"An army of miniature workers," Beaumont thought aloud with a tiny shrug, "that's a strange optical effect, I've never seen that before. I often think I'm flying over a rainforest when I look at broccoli on my plate but muesli is an absolutely different sort of food, one that should be immune to any misinterpretation. Ah well! It doesn't really matter, I will eat what is here anyway and I'll enjoy it. But my jaw feels strange, the upper and lower teeth aren't meshing in the right way."

He had difficultly chewing and when the ordeal was over he went to a mirror and opened his mouth wide at it.

Like a hippopotamus on a river, he decided.

But there was nothing inside of much interest, just a tongue and gums and a few shreds of dried papaya that resembled roses. Gums and roses, he intoned to himself like a mantra. He shut his mouth and wondered how to spend this weekend day in a profitable manner. He had been working so hard recently that he was unable to switch off. Agitation took hold of him and made his feet dance across the kitchen floor despite his efforts to shuffle instead. He needed to get out, despite the fact he had something wrong with his head, despite his anxiety.

Francine had taken the car, but the bicycle was in the garage. He took it and began pedalling slowly down the drive, then out onto the street and because he had no particular destination in mind he just allowed gravity to make the decisions for him. He freewheeled down a gentle slope to the end of the street, turned the corner and kept going. But at the base of the small hill he had to pedal hard to take him over the next rise. The roads were like that, undulating all the way from his house to the river. Then he knew that the river was his destination.

But what would he do when he got there? He had no special interest in rivers. He might watch the fishermen, if there were any around, for a few minutes, or wave at the passengers of a passing boat. Probably the only activity really available to him would be to pedal along the towpath to the nearest café and then order a coffee and sit doing nothing for one hour. Well, doing nothing in that sociable way was certainly better than doing nothing on his own at home, and if his head was going to change shape it might as well do so in public.

His tyres were a little flat, he should have pumped them up before he left his house, but it was too late to worry about that now. He felt every jolt in the road in the base of his spine and the impact seemed to travel up his backbone, from one vertebrae to the next, until it reached his brain stem, and the shock helped along the distortion of his skull, pushing it away from the roughly spherical shape it had always had into something sharper and with cleaner lines, he wasn't quite sure what, and he slowed down so the bumps would have less effect.

He reached the riverside at last and there was no one there, so it was pointless to linger and he cycled towards the café he knew so well, the one balanced on a jetty over the water itself.

"Good morning, Beaumont!"

He applied the brakes and looked around.

"Hello Harry," he said, "I'm sorry but I didn't recognise you."

"And why should that be?"

"You look totally different without the beard."

"That's not a good enough reason, Beaumont, not good enough at all, my friend. I recognised *you* even though there's something very different about you today, what can it be? Your features sit differently on your face for some reason, they are in new positions and have slid over your visage somewhat. But it makes no difference."

"No difference to whom?"

"Why, to me, of course, Beaumont, to me."

"Certainly, Harry, but—"

"No buts, my old pal, not buts and no ifs. I recognised you easily but you weren't able to pay me the same courtesy. That's disappointing but life is like that, I have come to expect such things. Let's say no more on the subject. Yes, I have shaved myself."

"Very closely too, Harry."

"Indeed. More closely than ever before!"

"And why is that, Harry?"

"The question ought to be *how*, not *why*, Beaumont. How? And it's not a difficult one to answer, not a difficult question at all, provided it is the right question. How? With a razor, dear sir, the sharpest razor that I have ever owned, a perfectly sharp razor."

"You bought a new one?"

"No, I did not, no and no again! I did not and I will not. No, the fact is that I took your advice, Beaumont. Yes, I followed your suggestion and it proved to be most efficacious. I am glad."

"I'm glad you are glad."

Beaumont blinked at his friend and thought that Harry didn't look too happy, certainly not as happy as he claimed to be, but this might also be a mirage, an illusion, just the same as the muesli had been, because without a beard it was possible to see the skin of Harry's chin and cheeks for the first time in years, and it was sallow, there's no other word for it, yellow and unhealthy and not suggestive of joy.

"I made a pyramid, Beaumont, I made one from stiff cardboard and it was of identical proportions to the Great Pyramid of Cheops, just as you said it ought to be, and I aligned it along the north-south east-west axis, very accurately, as you told me I should."

"It is always good to experiment," agreed Beaumont.

"Newton did! Galileo did!"

"You are in very fine company then, Harry."

His friend bowed deeply.

"Indeed I am, Beaumont, fine company indeed, and I must admit that my doubts about PYRAMID POWER are proven to be confounded. I should state unambiguously that I am now a convert, that I've changed my mind about the force I previously mocked."

Beaumont lifted his hand in a little wave. He was gratified to hear this but he was also eager to be on his way. Something about Harry's hairless face made him nervous, the smooth skin was like a repulsive forcefield, a form of animal magnetism pushing him away. His little wave turned into a gesture of determination, of kinetic intention, and he used the hand now extended to point towards his destination.

"I must be going," he said.

Harry nodded, then he lifted his own hands and rubbed them furiously over his face as if his face was a drowned child and his hands were towels and he was the rescuer. But he was aware that this attempt to return life to his features was futile. His face was dead. And Beaumont was already on his way, pedalling hard, grimacing excessively, breathing heavily, all this effort seeming to distort his head more.

He knew he ought to take it easy but there was a concentrated form of impatience inside him and he couldn't resist it. He felt the wheels rotating beneath him and for no good reason he began counting the revolutions. It is easy to become distracted when doing this. One, two, three, four, at the start the flow is smooth, five, six, seven, eight, then the revolutions go off on a tangent, French, Russian, Cuban.

The café he was heading for was called *La Jetée* and the fact it lurked and huddled at the end of a jetty was only part of the reason for the name. The owner was an intellectual, a culture vulture, a cinephile, and the inner walls of his establishment were plastered with posters from the beatified decades of avant-garde filmmaking. He liked to discuss obscure viewing experiences with his regular customers.

Beaumont dismounted and carefully wheeled his bicycle over rotting planks to the entrance of the café. He leaned it against a wall, not caring to lock it, and he entered the open door. Justin was leaning on the counter and reading a newspaper but his eyes swivelled upwards and he said with a drawl that wasn't really his own, "The usual, Beaumont?" But then his mouth curled up and he threw the paper down and added, "But it's rather an unusual Beaumont today, pardon me."

"I am a bit different."

"Have you had an accident, I wonder?"

"No, not one of those."

"Surgery of some kind? Cosmetic or cosmic?"

"Neither, I declare."

Justin gave up and attended to the coffee machine and poured one of the frothiest cappuccinos imaginable for Beaumont, who accepted it with a frown of pleasure because it creased his forehead therapeutically and a smile did not. The newspaper lay on the counter and the front-page story caught Beaumont's attention immediately. His frown remained fixed but its justification changed. There was a picture of his wife sitting in a salon chair and she was staring right back at him.

The headline announced: FRANCINE DECIDES TO HAVE BRAIDS. And the photograph confirmed the statement. "Well, well," Beaumont blinked, "I always assumed she would stay natural."

"But who?" Justin asked.

"Francine. I'm not complaining, it looks good, I'm just surprised, and it calls for another coffee, I think."

"What are you talking about?" Justin saw where Beaumont's eyes had lingered and he read the story too. "Yes, it looks like war is likely, but the region has always been prone to violence with diplomatic efforts liable to come to nothing. Is your chin hurting?"

"It just seems to be widening," insisted Beaumont.

"And without any pain?"

"None at all. Thanks for the cappuccino."

He pursed his lips to blow the excess froth off but they wouldn't purse properly, they were too rigid, constricted by horizontality, like the slots in doors that allow letters to pass from outside into a house. Then Beaumont knew his head was metamorphosing more rapidly than he had anticipated. He changed the subject, changed it back to the story of his wife's hair, but Justin still didn't understand, still saw war, no news of braids at all, just a photo of soldiers massing and marching.

"Are we reading the same page?" he demanded.

"The front page! The main story!"

Beaumont picked up the newspaper, fanned his ire with it, fanned the bafflement of the café owner, slapped it down again, pointed at the photo and then at the headline. But Justin saw an entirely different story, he saw preparations for a distant border conflict.

Beaumont fell back on his stool, clutched his skull.

"I must be seeing things!"

"Yes, you look ill, maybe you have fever."

Beaumont nodded and his nod felt strange, it felt solid and sharp, and then he fell back on his favourite topic, the one that had obsessed him for a year or more, the subject of pyramid power, and he said, "Did you ever try to preserve food like I suggested?"

"Had no time to make one of those contraptions."

"Fruit doesn't decay within."

"I believe you, but I'm a busy man, the café isn't doing so well, and I can't waste my days making cardboard pyramids. Sorry, if I ever have an hour spare I would rather watch a film."

"They work, they work well, that is all I wanted to say, and no matter how scientists try to dismiss the effects, the phenomenon is real. There's a mysterious power in the shape, a magic in the geometry. Razor blades can be kept sharp indefinitely. If you meditate inside one, your problems vanish, physical and emotional. Grapes became raisins in just a few days. Tarnished coins acquire a fabulous lustre."

"You've told me all this already, many times, and it's not that I doubt you but just that I'm not at all interested."

"Fair enough, no need to say more, how much?"

Justin charged him for only one coffee. "I prefer to help a sick man if I get the chance, and you are sick."

"Maybe I am, maybe I have an exotic disease."

"If the cappuccino fits, wear it."

"Good joke, nice joke, funny joke, clever joke."

It was none of those, but Justin smiled and said, "Thanks, Beaumont, I hope you get well soon, very soon."

Beaumont left, pondering. His ponders were deep, deeper, deepest, no stone cast into them would sink to the bottom before he returned home, so they were deeper than the water that flowed parallel to the first part of his route, and it really was water to be reckoned with, water that came from a remarkable distance, from melting snow.

He cycled slowly back along the path. Some children were swimming in the river. One of them shouted, "Pharaoh!" at him and the insult was so unexpected and recondite that he laughed and nodded, instead of snarling, and when he was far enough away from them, he braked and felt his skull all over, and yes, he understood the shout.

His head was a pyramid.

It was absolutely and unmistakably pyramidal.

Triangles meeting at an apex.

Isosceles triangles set at ninety degrees to each other, sloping steeply, smooth and cool to the touch and hairless.

Four of them, monumental.

The rapid transformation of his head was complete.

Everything now made sense.

But he wasn't able to appreciate the significance of what had occurred because too many people were staring at him, distracting him with laughs and hoots, as if he had pedalled into a zoo stocked with hyenas and owls and nothing else, and it was worse when he turned from the towpath and had to pedal on the road back to his house, the amplitude modulated sine wave hills slowing him down, people actually coming out of their homes to stand on the pavements and gawp.

"Mummy, why does that man have a head like a holy mountain? Is he the president of a secret society?"

"Don't be so immature, my son, my daughter."

"Is he sick, mummy?"

"Yes, or he is foolish, my children, or he is demented, or he is a form of troublemaker hitherto unknown in these parts, or he is an archaeological fraud, or he is a coincidence, or an actor. But don't call me mummy in his presence. You don't know what is inside that head of his. Call me mother instead. That's a much less risky word."

"Shoo him away, please!"

But he was already gone, wobbling all over the road, sweat cascading down his front slope and dripping in a liquid curtain from his chin, which was now the widest part of his head. Yet his brain was still churning over all sorts of ideas unrelated to his predicament. He was solving paradoxes in his mind, performing marvellous calculations, making odd connections between all sorts of distinct substances and events. His mind was ablaze, but with a supremely cool and dusty fire.

He reached his house and Francine was already home, despite the fact her hairstyle was now extremely complex, and this was because the salon prided itself on its incredible efficiency. She blinked at him as he entered and demanded, "Who on earth are you?"

"I am Beaumont, dear."

"But I didn't recognise you! Just look at you like that."

"Like what, sweetheart?"

"Like some sort of old Giza, that's what."

"I can't help it, honey."

She approached him and ran gentle hands over his head. "People will gossip about it and say you are—"

"A member of the Illuminati. I know, a child told me. But listen, there is nothing negative about this."

"Are you joking, Beaumont? It's a disaster."

He hugged her close and shook his head and it made a rumbling noise as if a very heavy building was shifting its foundations on the shrug of an earthquake tremor and then he said:

"No, it's a boon, a benefit, a blessing, really it is. I have been thinking about pyramid power, obsessing over it, and this is the result. My head is no longer natural. It has become what it was thinking about, it has gained all the qualities of a pyramid, and this means that my brain will be better, faster, more ingenious than before. Francine, you don't appreciate what a superior husband you now have. My brain and perhaps even my soul are inside the pyramid and subjected night and day to the focusing properties of its shape and thus they are evolving."

"Into what exactly?"

"Improved version of themselves, darling."

"As sharp as razors?"

"Yes, and perfectly preserved forever."

"This sounds like baloney and flapdoodle to me, Beaumont, like some sort of excuse for acting special. Those days have gone, and if you expect me to spend all my time looking up at you in reverence, then you need to find yourself another thought at once."

He held up his arms in a mollifying gesture. "Wait! Guess what I saw when I was in *La Jetée* earlier? A newspaper report about your braids! It was a form of precognition or remote viewing. My sharpened brain knew you were going to have braids, even though my conscious mind was still scoffing at the idea. And my pyramid-enhanced brain was right. Look at your hair, just look! See what I mean?"

Francine sighed and said, "But do you like it?"

"You look stunning, baby."

"Does it suit me?"

"Best hairstyle you ever had."

"Fine, I accept your judgement. This does prove you have a powerful mind inside that grotesque new head of yours. I am satisfied. But I don't see how you can go out and about like that. Maybe we ought to try a wig on you, or a big hat, or some sort of papier-mâché mask? Otherwise you are soon going to lose all your friends."

"Not Harry, he'll stay loyal. He's a convert now."

"Justin as well, I suppose?"

"He's always been very tolerant, café owners usually are. He has seen everything or nearly so, maybe not a man with a pyramidal head but other sights just as weird. Anyway, I can go out at night when there's no moon and keep myself to myself during the day. I'll have to get a job where I'm on my own all the time, security guard or something, but in fact I think it won't be hard earning money from home, because my intelligence will be enormous and surely highly profitable."

Francine chewed her lower lip. Then she shrugged.

"Very well, let's see how it goes."

That was the start of the period of Beaumont's life that he liked to call his Pharaonic Phase and he was happy with it. It really did seem that his intelligence increased every day and that he would eventually become the finest mind in town. But his income wasn't quite as substantial as he had promised it would be. Most of it came from solving crossword puzzles in newspapers and winning cash prizes.

His efforts to find a night job failed dismally. No employer wanted to hire a man with more than one facet to his personality, let alone his head, and they often berated or insulted him at interviews, asking him questions that were almost impossible to answer in order to make him fail. "What is the total number of atoms in a fence? How would you put handcuffs on a robber with three arms? What's the longest legally obligated leg?" But he was always polite in return, dignified.

"Something has been rummaging through our possessions," Francine said one morning when she was first up. "Look at the mess in the kitchen, all these broken plates and glasses on the floor. Can't you use your better brain to work out the cause of all this?"

Beaumont was still sleepy and replied, "Wait, honey."

"That's easy for you to say!"

"Not easy, darling, not easy at all. Saying anything at all takes such a mighty effort for me these days. My mouth is a slit that barely moves. I miss my old flexible jaw, I really do, and my smiles and frowns, they are like long lost friends, and eyeballs that roll, what a luxury! But I've come to accept my condition for what it is and I wouldn't change it for anything because I can think beyond any man."

"Burglars must have broken in while we were asleep."

"Are the windows smashed?"

"No, they are all intact, and none of the doors have been forced. That is what makes it so strange. And look!"

"What is it, Francine?"

"Tiny footprints in the spilled flour!"

Beaumont rolled out of bed and came to join her, still feeling groggy but unable to yawn with his stiff mouth. He blinked at the indentations in the white powder on the kitchen floor.

"They are human, but small, much smaller than the smallest man's. I think we were visited by a fairy."

"Fairies don't smash fine porcelain!" she cried.

"We don't know that yet."

An argument was about to begin, but Francine stooped and picked up something from the floor between index finger and thumb. It was a short length of miniature bandage, very yellow and crumbly, and it turned into dust while she was in the act of passing it to Beaumont. He winced. There was a sudden pain in his head, it felt as if something inside had cramp and had shifted position, and he wondered.

He stumbled out of the kitchen and made his way to the room that he had turned into his study. Here was the table at which he sat to solve his crossword puzzles. Francine called after him but he ignored her. He knew what was responsible for the damage in the kitchen but he dare not share his suspicions with his wife. She would blame him, even though it wasn't at all clear if he deserved such blame.

He rapped on the east side of his head with his knuckles.

"I know you are in there," he said.

It was his soul, perfectly preserved, dormant in its sarcophagus at the centre of his brain, wrapped in bandages and at peace with eternity. Yes, his soul had turned into a mummy, resting at the focal point of the mystic rays that were focused on it by the lenses of the pyramid sides. For some reason it had woken up last night and left his head, probably through his mouth, and gone on a rampage. Why?

A mummy usually awakens when its tomb is invaded and desecrated. Beaumont had seen enough films to know this. What had upset his soul in the middle of the night? Or could it simply be that his soul was a naughty one, that it was a swaddled mischief-maker and had no justification for its antics? Beaumont tore a piece of paper out of a notebook and he wrote a message on it with a pencil. IF YOU CAN READ THESE WORDS, RAP ONCE ON THE SIDE OF MY HEAD FROM INSIDE. Then he folded the paper and posted it through the letterflap of his thin mouth.

He waited but nothing happened. It was probably too dark inside for a mummy to read anything. Maybe the mummy of his soul could only read sentences in hieroglyphics? Perhaps the mummy didn't know how to rap and could only sing older forms of music? The experiment was a failure anyway, and it was better not to worry further about communicating with his soul and to just carry on as normal.

But the following night the mummy escaped again.

This time the damage was to the objects in his study and thus he took it much more seriously, and although Francine was furious too she also smirked at his discomfiture. She turned her head away quickly so that he wouldn't see her smirk and her long braids lashed him in the face like a whip, the whip of an overseer on a project. Not that the pyramids really were constructed with slaves, that's a myth. Paid workers were used like the flakes of oats, nuts and fruit in muesli.

His mind was wandering and he felt exhausted.

Clearly sleeping with an absent soul wasn't the most refreshing form of slumber and it left him vacant and sluggish and unable to concentrate on successfully completing his crosswords.

"Maybe you should beg the travel agency for your old job back," said Francine, "and tell them you've been ill."

"They won't have me."

"So what are you going to do?"

"They won't have me, dear. I resigned. I took my destiny into my own hands and here we are. Maybe I can ask Harry or Justin for help. Friends should support each other, after all."

"Yes," she said, "but after all isn't before all."

"What do you mean?"

"I mean that the trouble has only started."

And she was utterly right.

Beaumont's soul left his head every night and caused damage around the house. A week later he felt himself being shaken awake by his wife. It took him a long time to open his eyes and understand where he was. Then she said, "I saw it go back inside you."

"Sorry darling, what?"

"The miniature mummy. I saw it crawl through the slit of your mouth as if it was returning home after a party. It turned and looked at me and it made a rude gesture. I was too shocked to respond. I waited a minute and then I went to fetch the fly swat and I stood over your mouth but it didn't come back out. Still, there's no point trying to deceive me anymore. You have a mummy living in your head."

He admitted the fact to her and began to weep.

"There now," she crooned.

"I didn't ask for a soul that acts this way!"

"I believe you, honey."

"Don't hit it with a fly swat, please."

"I promise I won't."

"It might hurt and injure my soul forever."

She nodded sympathetically.

But he had to find a new job, she told him. He set off on his bicycle an hour later with a hood covering his head, which still retained its pyramid outline, but he felt more confident this way. He went down the hill to the river and along the towpath to *La Jetée* and found there not only Justin but Harry too. They smiled when he entered.

"The usual, Beaumont?"

"Please. It has been a really thirsty month."

"One capstone, I mean cappuccino, coming up! Drink and enjoy, for the café will be closing soon."

"You are taking a holiday, are you?"

"The business has failed."

There was an awkward silence. Beaumont looked around. There were no other customers and there were holes in the floorboards through which one could see the dark river flowing.

"Change the subject," announced Justin.

"My chin?" asked Harry.

"Smooth, smoother, smoothest," said Beaumont.

"You bet! Pyramid Power!"

"Pyramid Power!" bellowed Justin.

Beaumont couldn't bring himself to join the chant. He felt betrayed by the shape, the four triangles leaning together like conspirators or like lazy lovers kissing with polyamorous apex lips. He just raised a tired hand and let it fall to his side and his side welcomed it. But it occurred to him that if the café had been constructed in the shape of a pyramid to start with, it wouldn't have gone bankrupt now.

Justin either read his mind or had already been entertaining the same thoughts. "Yes, it can be remodelled and reopened. But that will require a great deal of money and I lack funds."

"Do you have any spare?" Harry leered at Beaumont.

"None at all. In fact I was—"

"You was what?" Justin leaned his elbows on the counter and glinted his eyes with contrived evil. "I asked everyone here to change the subject but clearly you want to talk money."

"Drink up," said Harry.

"Yes, drink up," echoed Justin.

"Have you laced my coffee with brandy?"

"Of course, my friend! Shoes can be laced, so what makes coffees so special they shouldn't be? That's just unfair. Have another and another. They are on the house, so don't fret."

Beaumont accepted and quickly became drunk.

"I had hoped to ask a favour from *you*," he finally admitted. "I need a job or a loan or advice or something."

Justin and Harry laughed and clapped their hands.

Beaumont kept drinking…

It was night and a cold wind was blowing.

He was outside. No, he was still inside the café but the walls had gone and so had the roof. They had collapsed into the river. He was quite alone at the very end of the jetty and clouds scudded high above, for he was on his back and his head was throbbing and there was a taste in his mouth as if he had swallowed the inner workings of the coffee machine that was no longer behind the vanished counter.

He staggered to his feet. His head felt empty and stuffed at the same time. He blinked and groped for his bicycle but it wasn't there. Someone had stolen it or thrown it into the river.

He would have to walk home.

It took a long time, the remainder of the night, for he took small steps and had to pause often for a rest. It was dawn before he reached his house and turned his key in the lock and entered.

Francine was waiting for him.

There were two men with her in the kitchen.

"Carter," one of them said.

"And I am also Carter," the other said.

Introductions over, they continued as before, sitting on stools, holding hands with his wife. Was this a séance? Were they police officers? It was impossible to be certain of anything.

"Darling, I phoned the university," said Francine.

The Carters nodded politely.

"We are archaeologists," they explained.

"It seems that all the best archaeologists must take the name Carter on the day they graduate," said Francine.

"It's an old tradition," added the first Carter.

"I phoned the university and described what had happened to you and these two gentlemen came around."

Francine beamed brightly. She was beautiful this morning, radiant, a flower in an oasis in a desert of chaos. Too good for me, Beaumont knew, and it was the first time he had known this since the moment he first saw her, all those years ago, this caramel angel on the steps of the library with her head buried in a book and the poetry dripping out of it like the juice of the peach she was holding in the other hand, taking alternate bites of culture with her eyes and fruit with her mouth, her flashing eyes and that lovely ripe mouth that smiled so well.

Those days were gone. That's what days do, they go.

Beaumont sighed. "What now?"

"Darling, they just want to open you up, take a look inside your head, see what's there. That's their job."

"We will compensate you fully," said Carter.

"In cash," said the other Carter.

"It's worth it, honey," said Francine. "We need the money. You said it yourself, we must do something."

Beaumont nodded. He was too weary to resist.

They asked him to lie down on the floor. He did so. One of the Carters had a spade, the other a pickaxe. The first blow hurt a lot but none of the subsequent strikes did. He tried not to whimper. Francine was standing over him and he wanted to be brave for her sake. Then one of the Carters knelt and groped inside the hole that had been made, groped as far as the elbow of his rolled-up khaki sleeve.

He felt around for a long time and slowly his expression under his pith helmet became one of brute dismay.

"It's empty. The tomb is completely empty!"

"No treasure?" cried Carter.

"Nothing at all! They even took the mummy."

"Tomb robbers!" wailed Carter.

They fell back and gnashed their teeth and shook their fists but when the fit was over they became serene again. The two archaeologists left without an explanation but it was obvious what had happened. Justin and Harry had raided Beaumont's head already. But how had they managed to do that without leaving marks that the archaeologists would have noticed? Then Beaumont remembered the razor.

Harry would have used his supremely sharp blade to remove mortar from between the blocks of stone in Beaumont's head. The blocks could then be slid out and access obtained to the inner chambers. The blocks would then be slid back and fresh mortar added in the form of cappuccino froth that would harden in a night wind.

"Darling, we still have each other. Doesn't that count for anything? I still think we can be happy," he rasped.

Francine looked down at him and smiled thinly.

"We'll see," she said.

Why Mummy is a Pharaoh

Gunther Doppeltroppel fled the city-state of Chaud-Mellé because of an earthquake that destroyed his house, and he wandered over icy mountains to the south until he arrived in Italy, where he settled in expectation of a quiet life. Seismic events were a rarity in his hometown and the incident deeply shocked him. His house had formed a mound of rubble in the shape of a pyramid.

He had walked around it, his frock coat white with dust, his tall hat crumpled into a flat cap from the impact of a falling brick.

"But this is unheard of!"

"Not so," spoke his neighbour, whose own home was leaning at a perilous angle but hadn't yet collapsed, "for in the annals of the city we can find accounts of ruinous earthquakes from other eras. For example, in the ninth century, the monk Flusterpots records tremors originating in the..."

This neighbour was a professor at the university.

"Bah!" snapped Gunther.

And he turned on the heel of his buckled shoe and immediately proceeded to quit the city of his upbringing. He was especially disturbed by the perfect symmetry of the pyramid of debris that his house had transformed into. There seemed to be something undeniably deliberate about the final shape.

The mountain passes were treacherous at this time of year and he nearly stumbled off the path on several occasions and once almost fell down a crevasse, but battered, frostbitten and snow-blind he finally staggered into the lowlands on the far side of the range. Then the going was much easier.

In Italy he was accepted, though not admired, and the terror in his bones started to subside. He had enough gold coins to pay rent on an apartment, to purchase a new hat and satisfy his culinary needs. He even allowed himself the indulgence of buying the daily newspaper and reading about distant affairs, including those of Austria, Prussia, Russia and occasionally Chaud-Mellé itself.

Then one day he received an unexpected visitor.

His peace of mind was shattered.

It was his mother, stooped and yet still taller than most other people, her hair tied in two pretzels on either side of her head, her lips more sensuous and ironic than the lips of any mother should be. She had a basket strapped to her back and in this wicker container were crammed all the possessions that had survived the quake but which he had abandoned inside that awful pyramid.

"Mother! How did you manage to track me down here?"

"I trusted to fate and chance."

"Come inside and have a glass of wine."

She grinned slyly at him.

He was appalled, yet remained polite. His manners had been conditioned from an early age and weren't easily corrupted. The Doppeltroppels prided themselves on the formal elegance of their behaviour. Gunther's late father had been even more polite, a man who said thank you to feral cats that scratched his face in dark alleys. As for his mother, Helga had the soul of a countess, even though there was nothing aristocratic in her lineage. Now she accepted the wine.

She sat on one of his chairs and asked, "Why didn't you say goodbye? Why didn't you let me know you planned to leave?"

"I assumed you were killed in the earthquake. You were inside the house when it collapsed. I walked around the rubble and examined it from every angle. The remains of the house had taken the form of a pyramid, a pyramid that had become your tomb. What is the point of bidding farewell to a crushed corpse? I couldn't take any more, my mind was in turmoil, my very soul seethed."

"So you ran away?"

Gunther nodded. How could he deny it?

"But I didn't die," she said.

"I see that now," he conceded, "but at the time..."

She drained the glass and held it up for a refill. He poured in the rosy liquid, fruity with a caramel aftertaste, that seemed to hold the sunlight in its depths even though it was a cloudy day and the interior of the house was rather dim. She licked those large lips of hers and then sighed with delight.

"Managed to crawl my way out, I did, and that's how I'm here today. Being in that tomb was weird, surrounded by the treasures of your youth, toys, books, ornaments. I felt unnaturally calm and almost decided to remain there. But I was too worried about you, that's a mother's instinct, and I scratched at stones with my fingers and emerged into daylight, and I resurrected myself."

"Praise be," intoned Gunther, though he wasn't religious.

"And now I hope we can..."

Her words were interrupted by a fearsome rumbling and shaking that threw them both off their seats and onto the floor. Chunks of masonry began falling around them and screams reached them from outside. Gunther began squirming towards the front door, which was dancing on its hinges, and just as he reached it, the way opened. He plunged through and only when he was in the middle of the narrow street, clutching the cobbles with all his might, did he spare a thought for Helga, his mother. Turning his head, he called out to her, but in vain.

The building in which his apartment was located had collapsed. He was lucky to have rented the ground floor. There had been insufficient time for the residents on the other floors to escape. The shaking ceased and he stood unsteadily, his ears ringing, a smell of burning in his nostrils. He was staring at a perfect pyramid and inside it was the corpse of his mother. Poor Helga!

But Gunther didn't weep. His first impulse was to flee.

He hurried through the crooked streets, climbing over obstacles that only minutes earlier been liveable structures, and he made his way to the quayside. To his immense relief, the harbour was still intact. The waters were choppy, surging from one side to the other, as if an invisible giant was taking a bath in them, and the few ships moored to jetties rose and fell like panting chests, but already this agitation was losing force, and Gunther was alert for opportunities.

He called to a captain who was standing on the deck of a swaying vessel with no more bother than if it were a steady marble plinth and he a statue in kinder lands with no seismic activity. He was swigging from a rum bottle and didn't answer Gunther at first. He had to drain the liquid to the dregs, a moral duty almost, before lowering the flagon and saying, "What do you want?"

"Are you sailing away?"

"I am drunk," answered the captain, "and that's why I didn't fall over in the quake. The rum fuddled me one way, the shaking another, and by some strange coincidence the two forces cancelled each other out."

"I'm sure it happens often. But my question remains."

"Aye, I am sailing soon."

"Will you take a passenger? I have gold coins."

"To Greece I am going. Have you been there? A country that ought to be like any other, but in fact it has a sprinkle of islands all around its feet, and that's not quite the way I prefer things to be. I am reminded of toast crumbs. When I eat my breakfast the same thing happens. Yet I'm sailing there."

"Then let me come too!"

The captain nodded brusquely. He had no real opinions about the look of Gunther either way. He was the drunkest captain on six of the seven seas and this is because the seventh was itself made from wine, or so he believed, and he didn't trust himself to explore it. Gunther Doppeltroppel was the only passenger. The crew ignored him. After several days they landed on an island.

Gunther decided to leave the ship here. He was unused to the sea, the motions of the waves reminded him too much of the undulating land during the two earthquakes, and his only desire was to find somewhere stable to settle down. Yes, even a stable, if it was solidly constructed, would suit him.

But as it happened he found a nice stone house to rent.

The island was named Thira and it was much more remote a home than Italy. The newspapers arrived by ferry once a week. This didn't bother Gunther, who now hated sudden or even rapid change. He ate olives and listened to the wind. He grew friendly with a woman who was a neighbour and romance might have blossomed one evening when they were sitting together under stars.

But then the shaking came and the trees in the garden fell down and the house lost control of itself and collapsed too, and a huge crack opened in the ground, and part of the island sheared off into the sea. The woman wanted to clutch him for comfort and threw herself in his direction to attain this aim, but he shrieked and fended her off. In his mind she was death coming to smite him.

His disordered imagination pictured her as congealed toxic vapours released from the depths that by chance had taken the shape of his beloved. He ran away with hands raised high, gibbering and drooling. He panted the length of the island and back again and when he returned he saw that his house was now a pyramid. He gnashed his teeth because that's what we do in such situations.

As he watched in disbelief, the stones at the base of this pyramid shifted a little. It was as if an occupant was trying to push one out. And in fact this is exactly what was happening. The stones moved again, with an effortful grinding sound, and a hole was revealed, and in the hole a crawling shadow. Was it his beautiful neighbour? But she had been in the garden with him all evening.

The shadow emerged, stood unsteadily and smiled weakly. A stooped figure, yet still taller than most, hair in spirals above the ears, lips erotic and sardonic but bloody and mashed too. It was Helga once again.

"Mother!" croaked Gunther.

"I brought your possessions with me from Italy. I mean those that survived," she gasped, and she lifted high the battered wicker basket that now contained only a few of the oddments and toys it had originally held. "Oh, that hurts," she added, "and my elbow appears to be somewhat mangled."

"But why?" he wailed.

"It was injured in the quake," she said.

"No, I don't mean that."

"You are referring to the toys? I brought them here because I assumed you might want them. They are your comforts."

"You misunderstand again. Why did you follow me here? What were you doing in my house without my knowledge?"

"You are my little boy, Gunther, and always will be."

"Please not now, mother."

"Are you ashamed?"

"I am wooing a woman. I have grown up."

"A dark haired lovely?"

"Yes, but most of the girls on Thira are that."

"With blue flecked eyes?"

"It's not common but not terribly rare."

"And pouting lips, almost as bulging and provocative as mine?"

"Yes, mother, but still…"

"That lady over there, with the chunk of masonry embedded in her skull? She lies dead now, drained of gore, but when I was trapped in the house I heard her screaming for an hour or more. It was terrible. She called your name, begged you to come to her aid. I wondered why you didn't. Ah well. That's life, I suppose. But take a look inside this basket. See what things remain!"

"How did you get inside the house? I am confused."

"I have been there for weeks, my son. I hid there. I was waiting for your birthday to come round, so I could jump out and surprise you. Only two more days to go. But that's not possible now. You have seen me. It doesn't matter. To track you down was difficult but I managed. Do you love me?"

"Of course I do," sighed Gunther, and he meant it. But his mind bubbled, popped, crackled with fearful thoughts. His mother had followed him from Italy to Greece, as she had followed him to Italy from Chaud-Mellé. He adored her in many ways, but it was beginning to feel as if he was bonded to her with unnatural fetters. He burst into tears. The moon rose and cast the shadow of the pyramid that had once been a house towards him. Its apex jabbed his chin.

"Don't cry, my sweet scion," his mother crooned.

"I can't stay here. Another quake might happen at any moment! I disliked tremors before, but now I am utterly terrified."

"Once I heard it said that there are very few or no earthquakes in Africa. Why not settle on that massive continent, dear boy?"

"But you will follow me..."

"No, no, I promise I won't. I won't follow you. Go ahead and leave with my best wishes. I appreciate what it's like to have an acute phobia. You are scared of the land when it shudders. I am terrified of ducks. It has always been this way. Irrational but intense nonetheless. Who am I to judge?"

Gunther hurried forward to kiss his mother's outstretched hand. Then he turned, a new determination coursing through his soul. He would go to Africa! It was time for him to make an extra-large effort, yes indeed. He didn't doubt Helga's assertion that it was a place without earthquakes. He had never known her to lie, except on that single occasion when she insisted that one of her ancestors had been a teapot. And even that might be true in some metaphorical way.

He felt himself tugged by an odd gravity. He had to climb down the latitude lines as if they were the rungs of an immense ladder, or else he would fall and dash out his brains at the base, wherever that might be.

In fact it was a few days before he could find a vessel willing and able to take him there, and the cost of his passage was high. But the voyage was uneventful and suited his fragile nerves. They docked in Alexandria, a port full of coffee shops that smelled of perfume and brothels that smelled of coffee. He strolled the esplanade and decided he had found his true home. He rented an apartment and breakfasted each morning on a balcony overlooking the mazy old town.

He felt secure and began to relax. He frequented a coffee shop on the waterfront. It became his regular haunt, a place where customers of many nationalities gathered to read newspapers, listen to the musicians, conduct business deals, swap saucy photos, argue politics, and explain recent military campaigns with the aid of plates of falafel or baklava. Gunther contributed to all this.

One day the place was full of a team of archaeologists who were about to embark for Cairo. It was fascinating to overhear them. At last Gunther introduced himself and said, "You are interested in pyramids for professional reasons, but I have only hatred for the shape. Three of the buildings I lived in collapsed into miniature pyramids, so I distrust that particular geometry. The pyramids of Egypt are still standing after many centuries because there are no quakes here."

One of the archaeologists shook his head ruefully. "That's intriguing but not quite right, my friend. Alexandria has experienced several powerful earthquakes in history. The scientific reason why pyramids never fall down is because they are in the shape of a building that has *already fallen down*, namely a pyramid shape, which is the final resting position of loose rubble and debris."

Gunther was horrified. "You mean to say there is a risk of seismic activity in this city too? But what am I supposed to do?"

"If you don't care for earthquakes, then come with us. The further south you travel in this country, the smaller the chances of being caught in one. Cairo is less prone to them than Alexandria. We are leaving today."

"Is this a serious offer?"

The archaeologist nodded and grinned. "My name is Carter. Pleased to have you along. Permit me to introduce my colleagues. This is Carter. And this chap over there is Carter. On that other table are Carter, Carter and Carter. As for Carter, he went out for a newspaper but he'll be back soon. The other Carters are in the brothel. With the exception of Carter, who doesn't do such things. We have a very important job to do when we reach Cairo. Something radical."

Gunther was overwhelmed. He hurried back to his apartment to pack a small bag. He was ready to leave when the archaeologists were, and he rode in one of the several jeeps that the team had at their disposal. He sat in the front passenger seat next to the driver, Carter, and in front of three other Carters. They rumbled and spluttered out of Alexandria and Gunther asked a question.

"Are there any archaeologists who are not named Carter?"

Carter laughed. "Very few," he said.

"Only mavericks or renegades or fools," added one of the Carters in the back and that was that. The ways of the world are strange indeed, Gunther told himself, and he didn't probe for more details. He tried to enjoy the trip, but the landscape was far too harsh for his taste, so he closed his eyes and wallowed in memories of his childhood. He pictured himself playing a big tuba in the annual Nut Festival on an elevated stage while that year's Harvest Queen kept time on his testicles with a soft mallet. This was an ancient custom with mysterious origins.

Then he frowned. The pain in his loins had been pyramid shaped, had it not? Not that pain has a definite topology, but something bothered him about this memory. His happiness was spoiled by a trepidation that all was not as it should be, and that things were nightmarish at all times below the surface. The surface of what? He was jolted awake by a bump in the desert road. He had been sleeping. He opened his eyes. The jeep was nosing itself through a sandstorm.

"Won't be long now," said Carter.

"The journey is almost over?" Gunther mumbled.

"No, I was referring to the jeep. It was originally rather a long vehicle. Each time we pass through a sandstorm, the flying grains erode some of our length. Finally we are just the size of a normal automobile."

"These sandstorms are abrasive rascals," declared another Carter.

"You can shave by them," confirmed Carter.

"Unless you are a truly hairy bastard, that is," said Carter.

"And strop yourself on howls."

This obscure banter was too much for Gunther Doppeltroppel to digest. He wasn't of this fraternity and perhaps they were reminding him of the stark fact. He was still a denizen of that mountain republic, where snowmen were allowed full citizen rights if they were constructed well enough, and even awarded medals on occasion. And now he was in a land of penetrating light and camels. He decided to say no more, and sat in a fudge of his own silence until Cairo.

They entered the city and circled a large roundabout a dozen times at high speed, to throw rivals off their scent, as one of the Carters explained to him. Gunther wanted to know more. "There are archaeologists from other nations," came the reply. "They are very voracious," said another Carter.

Now they headed off down a maze of narrow streets, zigzagging a route anxiously, and suddenly a jeep roared out at them from a false house front. It was a large sheet of paper painted to look like all the other buildings and the jeep burst through it with a tearing sound that ripped apart Gunther's soul. Carter accelerated but this other jeep drew parallel with them, and in this manner they cascaded along ways that were only just wide enough for both vehicles, scraping their sides on stone walls. Gunther saw grinning faces behind very grimy windows.

"It's that team from Germany!" bellowed Carter, and when Carter asked him if he recognised any of them, he nodded. "I think I caught a glimpse of Schliemann. Met him at a conference last year. He is sitting on the back seat between Schliemann and Schliemann, who I know from photographs in archaeology journals. They may try to throw sausages at us. Take evasive action!"

Carter slammed on the brakes, wrestled with the gear stick and put the jeep into a screeching reverse. The rival team kept going, the momentum of their glee too great to arrest. Then Carter found a junction where he could turn, and he rumbled off in the other direction. The zigzagging continued but eventually they pulled into a compound with a sentry where they parked and eased their stiff bodies out of the uncomfortable seats. The headquarters of their organisation.

"Let's have tea and anecdotes," said Carter, taking Gunther by the arm and leading him through a series of oddly shaped empty rooms to a chamber in the exact centre of the compound. "One lump or two?"

"I prefer coffee," ruefully admitted Gunther.

"Ah yes, it takes all kinds of personalities to make a world. Consider the Germans we had a close brush with just an hour ago. Carter here would have us believe that to hurl sausages at us is the only thing they care about. But that is stereotypical rubbish. Yet I still admire Carter for his work with scarabs. Do you understand? We must stay together in this land. In unity is strength."

Gunther nodded, not knowing what else to do. Then he asked, "What projects are you intending to work on next?" And most of the Carters rubbed their chins as if they were uncertain of the wisdom of telling him too much. The chin rubbing continued as the tea and coffee were brought on a silver tray by a Carter who wore a fez and a long white robe. At last Carter came to a decision.

"I think we can trust you. There's something about your face that inspires faith in the purity of your inclinations. Remember how I said that a pyramid has the shape of a building that has fallen down? After long research, we have come to the conclusion that the pyramids weren't constructed in the forms they presently have. We now think they were originally some other kind of structure, but that some force, maybe a quake or a monster, knocked them over. Well, now."

He paused and one of the other Carters took over. "Our daring plan is to turn them back into the buildings they once were."

"With hired labour to help, of course," said Carter.

"We could never manage to shift such massive stones on our own," added Carter with a snort. "We are manly, yes, but also exquisite, and there are certain limits. There are limits to most things. As for yourself..."

"You may join the work force. The wages are reasonable."

Gunther felt sweat bead his brow.

"But I am not suited for physical exertion," he pointed out. "Look at me! I am a cultured man, quite indolent, prone to romantic wistfulness, dreamy and fanciful. My father was an extreme pacifist. He never encouraged me to attempt strenuous activity. My mother always sheltered me as if I was fragile. I have gold coins, many of them. I am hoping to live on my inherited wealth."

Carter exchanged amused glances with Carter and Carter.

And spoke in a kind and soothing voice:

"That kind of money is not legal tender here, my friend. The only currency that is valid in shops and banks is lapis lazuli. We will pay you in lapis lazuli. You will work for us. You will be happy, learning how to manhandle stones in the sun. Oh yes! And consider the immense satisfaction you will feel at contributing to the most important archaeological program of the century! You have very little choice, to be blunt. If we remove our protection what will happen?"

"The crocodiles will weep for you," said another Carter.

"Like young girls," smiled Carter.

"Also, you hail from the mountainous city-state of Chaud-Mellé, which is not far from Germany. How do we know you aren't a spy working for Schliemann? A sneaky infiltrator who is determined to sabotage our scheme? But we trust you, as we have already made clear. Now you must trust us."

"Or come to a sticky end."

"And be abandoned far out in the burning barren sands."

"Well, what do you say?"

Gunther found himself unable to say anything, but he nodded. This mute gesture was sufficient to change the communal mood of the Carters. They applauded him and ordered more coffee, with little cakes, and even asked if he wanted to watch a shadow play about a dancing woman dressed only in bangles, but he was in a state of shock. So they led him to the guest bedroom instead and he collapsed on an iron cot, fell into a deep instant sleep, and that was entirely that.

When he woke the next day his new unpleasant life began. They drove him out to the site of the Great Pyramids, where he joined thousands of other workers, and then he was allocated a squad and set to work breaking up the immense structure that was the largest pyramid of all, the tomb of Cheops. Large screens had been erected around the site, to conceal this dismantling work.

But as the Carter who acted as their foreman informed them, they weren't really dismantling it, because it had never been constructed that way. When all the separate parts were laid out on the desert floor, he went on to say, it would soon be clear how they ought to be connected, and the resultant shape surely wouldn't be pyramidal but something else. The exciting part of the mystery was in wondering what this original shape could be. Carter enjoyed speculating.

"It might be a perfect sphere," he said, "or a rearing sphinx with a sad expression. Or an edifice twisted in a tight spiral. Maybe it will be a lighthouse with a stone eye at the top instead of a lamp. It could be anything. It might even," and here he lowered his voice to a whisper, "be in the shape of Carter."

"Which one?" rasped Gunther.

Carter shrugged. "Any. Does it really matter?"

Gunther leaned on his spade.

"I don't understand why the Egyptian authorities are allowing you to do this to the most important historical structures in their country. And why don't the Schliemanns try to disrupt our work? We are sitting targets out here. I don't seriously believe those screens will keep them out for long."

Carter smiled thinly. "Keeping the project secret has been the toughest part so far. We paid enormous bribes to government officials to let us do what we liked. And the Germans have been thrown off the scent by mechanical means. On the other sides of the screens we are projecting images of the intact pyramids. The deception is working well so far. We have outwitted our rivals." He paused for effect. "Mind you, wouldn't it be ironic if the reassembled pyramid turns out to be an immense sausage?" Then he laughed and cracked his whip. "Back to work!"

The days passed in a slick of sweat and Gunther was soon burned to a crisp by the relentless sun. He fell ill with heatstroke and was laid to recover in a tent hospital also on the site. He raved in his delirium and foamed at the mouth. At the end of each day, tired and grimy workers came to wash themselves on the froth of his lips, for this was the only bubble bath available in the locale.

By the time he was strong enough to think clearly again, the pyramid had not only been taken apart but put back together in a different configuration. It was very late in the afternoon when he lurched to the flap of the tent and peered out. Gunther blinked. In the twilight the edifice loomed like an angel of death, as high as a tall tower but as broad as a meeting hall. And yet in shape it was a house and a house that was awfully familiar to him. He stifled a scream of joy.

Or it might have been a scream of despair, he wasn't sure. For standing before him in early starlight was a gigantic replica of his house in Chaud-Mellé, the home he had shared with his parents for so many years. His house had collapsed into a pyramid but now this pyramid had been turned back into his house. It was beautiful and shocking. He clapped his blistered hands and grunted.

The other workers were trudging to their own tents to rest their weary limbs. The Carters were sipping pink gin and doing whatever else they did in the clubhouse they had erected with spare stones. There was nothing to stop Gunther stumbling forward and approaching the house. The front door was bigger than his entire original house, the handle far out of reach, but it was ajar. It was easy for him to slip inside and even as he did so he wondered what he was doing.

"There is something bad here," he said to himself, and he blinked. For there in the main downstairs room stood a dreadful figure. It was his mother, hugely magnified, a smile of sincere affection on her face. Despite her stoop, she was taller than the tallest steeple of any cathedral he had seen. Her hair mimicked a pair of distant galaxies, one over each ear. Her speech was a thunder rumble.

"I trusted to fate and chance."

"But mother!" Gunther Doppeltroppel was shouting at the top of his voice, yet his words were like motes of dust in a stadium. "You promised not to follow me. On that island you made the promise. Yes, you did."

Her smile remained in place. It was an inverted rainbow drained of colour. A vast but desiccated curve, the horizon of an imploding planetoid. Now he noticed that she was swathed in cobwebbed bandages.

"I kept my promise. I didn't follow you. I was already here. I have been here for a dozen millennia. Waiting for you, my son."

Then she held out massive arms for an impossible embrace.

"Waiting for you. Just for you."

Ponzihotep

Francine was in an aeroplane and enjoying the world as it rolled below. Her sister had invited her to stay for a few months and Francine had packed a bag and headed to the airport after kissing Beaumont farewell. He wasn't allowed to protest. She hadn't seen her sister for years. Now she was in her seat with her nose pressed to the window and trying to imagine that distant northern country that was her destination. The seat next to her was occupied by a man who said:

"And now we are passing over Madagascar."

She knew and didn't reply.

But he kept telling her where they were in relation to the ground and before long his voice became like turbulence, an irregular and brief change in the space that was now hers. It wasn't annoying enough for her to complain. It was somehow inevitable, an intrinsic part of the immediate environment of the passenger section of this nearly miraculous vehicle. It washed her ears.

"That's Sudan down there. Can you see the confluence of the Nile?"

She could, and it was remarkable.

The aeroplane was flying in that graceful curve that passes for a straight line on a flat map. From her own island in a warm ocean to another island in cold waters. She read several books. Then the man said:

"Do you know what city that is? That string of lights?"

It was night. She shook her head.

"Alexandria," he muttered. It was like a necklace on the continent. Then he sighed and added, "Named after whom?"

"Alexander the Great," she replied automatically.

"Not so! Andria is the answer."

"Who was Andria?"

"Andrea is my wife. She left me."

"And you are Alex?"

"That is right. The city reminds me of what we had. It mocks me. But I am being fractious and silly. Forgive a sentimental fellow." He offered his hand for a shake. "I know it's a bit late to introduce myself. Alex Carter. I am travelling on business. It's a long flight but not a very wide one."

She said nothing in response. She felt sorry for him. They continued over a set of other countries, the patchwork states of Europe, the obscure mountain republics full of curious festivals and clock towers.

She slept and when she awoke they were over the sea again. "The Faroe Isles," he said. It was very early morning. She drank her breakfast coffee and watched as those lumps of rock receded into the distance.

"Is that where pharaohs come from or go to?"

"Different spelling," he said.

"So they have nothing to do with dead kings?"

"Very little, I'm afraid."

"Don't be afraid. I suppose our flight will soon be over."

"A few more hours," he agreed.

They landed and disembarked and Francine forgot about the man. Her sister was waiting for her inside the airport. She had a small car and drove Francine the short distance into the city and to her apartment block. "And how is Beaumont?" she asked with no genuine concern in her voice.

"He has a sore head, but otherwise he is fine and trying."

"Trying what exactly?"

"Trying hard. To please me."

Then Francine smiled to herself with affection. He was lovable as well as foolish, funny as well as exasperating.

"It's a shame he couldn't come with me, but I am glad to see you."

"Have you been busy?"

"Yes. You wouldn't believe it. But let's save that kind of talk for later. I am hungry and tired and I need a shower."

Francine's sister was called Iris and her apartment was small, neat and clean. The capital of this country was a brightly coloured and quirky place but there was a sense of brooding underneath the surface. In winter the climate must have been unbearably harsh, and yet people bore it, so maybe not. The local inhabitants were mostly yellow haired and tall with very pale skin. People are people are people, Francine told herself unnecessarily. She didn't care at all.

"Regard my home as your own," said Iris.

Francine was grateful to her.

Over the following days they caught up on news, shared observations about life. It was like old times back in the tropics, in that house with the corrugated iron roof and the coconut palms all around it. Iris gave Francine a tour of the city and a big part of the island too. It was bleak and dramatic and an odd contrast of severe and bubbling with thermal springs dotted at various locations. They bathed in several and Iris tried to explain the geology of these volcanic vents wholly in terms of their physical health benefits, then she added, "But that's not all."

"What do you mean?"

"Just concentrating on physical health." Iris waved a dismissive hand. "That's not good enough. What about our mentalities?"

"I am sure that relaxation is good for the mind too."

"Not as good as security."

"I feel very secure here," Francine said.

"Organic security."

Francine waited for Iris to explain, but she fell silent instead and that was that for the day. It wasn't until the following week that she elaborated on the statement, quite unexpectedly one afternoon over lunch.

"I'm part of a scheme."

"Oh yes?" Francine forked an expensive imported olive and examined it. Like the jewel in an ancient crown, she decided.

"I am very excited. It's a great opportunity for me."

"I'm pleased to hear that."

"Not just for me," she added, smiling blandly.

"But listen. Does it involve money? Do you have to give someone your savings? I worry about such things. Oh, I mean, there are all sorts of frauds being perpetrated in society. Don't fall for any charlatans, please."

"It doesn't involve money, no."

"Well, that's good. That's very good, isn't it?"

"I just have to *recruit* people."

"For what exactly?"

"Two people to be precise. Everyone who joins has to recruit two more. That's the way the scheme keeps expanding."

"Yes, but the purpose of the scheme is what?"

"You ought to join."

And Iris refused to say more on the topic, but Francine was a little alarmed. Later she telephoned Beaumont and told him, not to get advice, which was sure to be weak and poor, but for the relief occasioned by pouring out her doubts into his ear at such a long distance. The line was bad, it crackled and hissed. Francine felt the conversation was spanning aeons as well as leagues.

"I guess she knows what she is doing. She's an adult."

That was Beaumont's wisdom.

Francine said goodnight, put the telephone down and stared into space. Her swift departure returned to her, the sudden decision to take a vacation, the night of passion before the day of her flight, an attempt to rekindle a connection that had been slowly slipping for a long time? Organic security. Those had been the words Iris had used. I lack that too, Francine decided. But what was it? The term was too vague and echoes of its meaning were too faint to decipher.

Rather oddly, Francine soon forgot all about the mysterious scheme of her sister and more days passed innocently enough. She visited restaurants, galleries and a few nightclubs, most very expensive, and went on a bus tour of the circumference of the island. She read lots of books too.

One of these was a controversial volume on archaeology. The author pointed out that to the Ancient Egyptians the magic verses painted on the walls of their tombs and the rituals that went with them were designed to keep their souls intact in an afterlife. The moment their identities were forgotten on Earth they would begin to fade away in the next world too. A double death.

For millennia the tombs had been buried by sand, the names of the occupants lost to history. So they had died twice. But archaeologists had opened up those tombs in recent years, had decoded the spells in the hieroglyphs, had spoken the magic words, brought the names back from oblivion, rescuing their owners from nonexistence. In other words the afterlife was suddenly full of them again. They had been gone a long time but now were back. This might annoy other ghosts who might feel crowded. The archaeologists would be held responsible.

The author concluded that the job was thus a dangerous one and he recommended that young people study some other subject at university. Francine finished the book and wondered if she believed in ghosts. Even if they did exist, she thought, they can't ever be annoyed by anything because annoyance is a physical condition. It requires a raised blood pressure and the release of adrenalin and ghosts don't have any of that. It didn't seem so hazardous an occupation after all, at least not for that reason. Blocks of stone falling on you were a bigger risk.

A silly book. She read another, but it turned out to be even more farfetched. This author claimed that the Trojans had invented time machines and had utilised them to travel back in time to the beginnings of Egyptian civilisation in order to manipulate history and make mischief. The evidence was compelling, the book insisted, but that was a matter of opinion, Francine concluded. Only one line in the volume struck her as memorable: "Pyramids aren't pyramids."

But in that case, what were they? The book didn't answer that question. Why Iris had such a collection of works on her shelves was the biggest mystery. Her new life in this northern city must have changed her personality. Then Francine remembered the 'scheme' and wondered about that too.

Iris finally took the plunge and divulged her secret to Francine. It happened over a breakfast of muesli and yoghurt one morning. She said, "I have recruited one person. I just need to recruit one more."

"I'm not stopping you," replied Francine.

"Well, you aren't yet, that's true. But if you decline to be recruited yourself, then I think I'll be justified in saying that yes, you are stopping me. So the question remains. Will you agree to be my second recruit?"

Francine put down her spoon with finality so that it clicked on the rim of her bowl like a metal tongue in a monster's jaw. "You haven't explained what you are recruiting me *for*. What am I supposed to do in this scheme of yours?"

"I told you. Recruit two more people."

"But what else?"

Iris was bewildered. "Nothing else."

"No, my dear, that makes no sense at all. The world doesn't work like that. If I am only required to recruit two people who are only required to recruit two people and so on, it won't be long before the entire population of humanity is recruited, for no good purpose. Everything will be the same."

"Nothing is ever the same, Francine. You must know that."

"Ever the same as what?"

"As anything, of course! You are in a funny mood."

"But tell me. Who recruited you?"

"One of my friends."

"And who recruited them? Can you see what I'm getting at? I am hoping to work back to the origin of this domino effect."

Iris pursed her lips and frowned. "I've never really thought about it. I suppose we might make enquiries. But–"

Francine returned to her breakfast and concentrated on chewing. A few days later Iris pestered her again. This time Francine gave in to impulse and said, "Very well, I will be your new recruit. Are you happy?"

Iris was. But now Francine was left with the task of recruiting two others. Could she manage to do this on the telephone and rope Beaumont into the mysterious plot? Undoubtedly. But that felt like cheating somehow. She thought about Alex, the man who had sat next to her on the flight.

She decided to track him down. That shouldn't be too hard. It was a small country and she knew his name and he was here on business, so he had to be staying in one of the big hotels here in the capital. She was also determined to find out the true purpose of the scheme and who had started it. That might be more difficult. She asked Iris to introduce her to the person who had recruited her and Iris reluctantly did so. This was a man named Lars. He was friendly enough. They met for coffee and Francine told him about her mission. He agreed to help.

Over several weeks she traced the sequence back in time to the earliest recruits on the island. Some of these people were more affable to her than others, but none were nasty or refused outright to give her the names of the previous link in the chain. They had nothing to gain, true, but nothing to lose. She bought them coffee. It was enough to oil their tongues. But mixing only with those who were already recruited, Francine found it impossible to win her own recruits.

"You've missed your chance," Iris told her one day.

"What do you mean?"

"Everyone on the island is part of the scheme now. The very last individual agreed to be recruited one hour ago. It was on the news. The entire country is part of a thing that's bigger than any of us. We don't know what that thing is yet. But we are going to find out. A gathering is being arranged."

Francine was troubled but she couldn't say why.

She had one more person to meet for coffee, the very first to be recruited into the scheme. The second person to be recruited would also be able to reveal the identity of the ultimate mastermind of this insane scheme, because both had been recruited from the same source, but Francine felt it was neater to get answers from the first domino. There was something about that metaphor she didn't like. She hadn't played the game since she was a little girl. No, it was more like music, a melody line, two note chords that had multiplied into a complex harmony.

Bjorn Wakeman had sleepy eyes and even four cups of coffee didn't seem to wake him from a daze, but he was lucid enough when she asked him direct questions. The man who had recruited him had done so via a letter. Bjorn was under the impression that thousands of these letters had been circulated, sent to random addresses in many different countries. The letter was from someone named Gunther Doppeltroppel. That was all Bjorn could tell her. The letter had asked him to win two recruits and that they in turn must recruit two more. And so on. He had done so because he had nothing else to do and it seemed it might be fun.

"And now there are no recruits left," said Francine.

Bjorn shrugged and smiled.

But the news had exaggerated as always. There was in fact one person who wasn't a part of the scheme. He had resisted all attempts to recruit him. Alex Carter. And the way that Francine discovered this was by bumping into him in the supermarket one evening. "Remember me?" she said.

"Of course. We flew over many countries together."

"How many exactly?"

"Eighteen. But that doesn't mean much."

"I was hoping to see you again. I have something to ask you. A favour, if you like. I am a member of a scheme and—"

"Oh no, no," he said, grinning and holding up his hands as if to fend off a physical assault. "I have no intention of joining the cult. In fact it's a requirement of my sacred calling that I remain outside it."

"Do you really believe it is a cult then?"

"Absolutely. What else?"

He seemed surprised that she had joined and in his frown there were questions for her. Did she understand what the gathering would involve? The whole setup might be innocent at the moment, but that was shortly about to change. She didn't have to fear that she would be cheated of her money. That wasn't what it was about. No, it was a much stranger affair, but he couldn't give her precise details of what to expect. There would be a strong geometrical aspect to it, of that much he was sure. How the aspect would be applied was a different question.

"Your sacred calling?" she said.

"My business. I came here on business. This is it."

"What are you exactly?"

"An archaeologist. Didn't you know? We are all called Carter. I specialise in what my colleagues refer to as *displaced pyramidology* but which has no official name. It's a new subset of the discipline of archaeology. There are pyramids in many places, not just in Egypt. The assumption that pyramids are inherently Egyptian is simply untrue. There are remarkable pyramidal structures in Nubia, in the Canaries, in Mexico and Guatemala, in Peru, in the Balkans, in Tibet, possibly in Antarctica. They can be any size or colour. Some have appeared in gardens, in kitchens, in the shape of teardrops wept by moonlit maidens, in tumours, in badly risen loaves of bread, in mushrooms or bedsheets. Some ghosts adopt a pyramid form, no one knows why. Vegetables and fruits have been contorted. And there are schemes like this one. Pyramid Schemes. I investigate them. I observe and report."

"You regard that as *sacred?* But it's just a job."

He shook his head. "No."

Then he softened and added, "I am a Carter. For us, archaeology is a faith as well as a means to make a living. We are like funky monks. We take a vow of service. The spade is our holy symbol. The pyramid is the womb of our faith. Naturally we always investigate Pyramid Schemes but we don't interfere before the pyramid is created. To do so would be putting the Carter before the Horus, as the saying goes. We stay out of things until it's time to force entry."

"What do you know about Gunther Doppeltroppel?"

"A certain amount," he said.

"Would you be good enough to tell me some of it?"

"He worked for many other Carters once. He comes originally from the mountain republic of Chaud-Mellé. We flew over it. But he has travelled extensively. He wears a flat cap that was originally a tall hat. He invented the scheme that you wanted to ask me to join. He has set up similar schemes in almost every country in the world. When the entire population of a nation has joined it, more or less, he will activate it. That is my belief anyway. This island is his first success. Every inhabitant has joined. But at present I believe he is only experimenting, that he is hoping to perfect some methods that will enable him to embark on a much grander version of the scheme. I just don't know what that is yet. At the moment I am a neutral. If something happens that needs action I will take that action."

"The scheme is why you are here?"

"Yes. I have been waiting. Waiting for something to happen. I couldn't anticipate what it might be. I still can't. But soon."

"Should I be worried?"

He considered the question deeply. "I don't know. Gunther Doppeltroppel is quite an unusual man. Something happened to him. He had a peculiar experience in Egypt that disordered his mind. He came to believe that pyramids were originally buildings with a different shape. This horrified him. Now he does his best to fill the world with new pyramids, to cover the surface of the globe with pyramids, to *pyramidize* reality, if I may be allowed to invent that word."

"You may," she conceded.

"Thank you," he said.

He left it at that and said no more. He regarded Francine as a lost cause, one who had already given herself to the scheme. She was a part of it and he was here merely to observe and record, not to intervene. He wouldn't engage deeply with her, despite feeling a connection, maybe an attraction that was more than physical. At the same time he understood that she was intrigued by him but not aroused in the slightest. He was a key to a locked door in her path. But that was fine, that was how it should be. I am not here seductively, he told himself.

Understanding that no more words could be extracted from the tomb that was his mouth, Francine said farewell, proceeded with her shopping and made her way back to the apartment of her sister. Beaumont had rang and left a message for her. He had whitewashed the exterior of their house.

"Trying very hard, isn't he?" Iris was in a buoyant mood.

"Bless him," said Francine.

"The gathering will take place in the very centre of the island. That's quite a neat idea, don't you think? Very symmetrical and fair. This island is very different from the island where we grew up. It is ordered."

"Ordered? Do you like following orders?" Francine said.

"You know what I mean."

The time for the designated gathering soon arrived. Iris drove Francine there on a road that was full of other vehicles going to the same destination, cars, buses, lorries, motorbikes and bicycles. They trundled along in this unexpected convoy and finally crested a rise to the top. Now they had a view of the plain below and the sight was a remarkable one. Vehicles stood abandoned and people were rushing on foot, stripping off their clothes as they did so, running to join a mass of writhing nude flesh that was already several thousand bodies strong.

"All those naked men and women!" Francine was shocked.

"This must be the reason," said Iris.

"The reason for what?"

"The scheme! But it's not an orgy. I just don't get that impression at all. I bet it has a mystical significance. Let's find out."

She opened her door and climbed out before Francine could restrain her. Then she was running and shedding her garments. Francine followed to drag her back, but the magnetic attraction of the growing mountain of bodies pulled her along too, and now she found her own clothes peeling off.

Some sort of hysteria was overcoming the participants. They were impatient to be a part of the growing tangle of bare humanity. Before Francine reached the outer edge of the trembling mass she understood that it was growing into a pyramid, that as more and more layers of people were added, its sides would slope to a point. The very last person to join would become a capstone.

Was that an honour or not? She didn't know. It was too late for her, the current of madness had caught her with irresistible force, though a part of her mind was lucid, a sober observer of the bizarre process. A pyramid that consisted of every inhabitant of this country, made from blocks of life instead of stones, living, breathing, quivering, sweating, shivering, shuffling along on hundreds of feet, moving in random patterns over the island, a gestalt being, unwise.

And now she was inside it, swimming through knots of arms and legs, under the blissful smiles of celebrants, her tiny image reflected in glistening eyes, gravitating towards the very heart of the mound, as if that was her rightful place. It grew dark as the surrounding bodies blocked the light.

She was inside a chamber made from curving backs and arching limbs. This was her resting place. She would await rebirth here, or something along similar lines, she didn't know what, nor how it might occur.

She felt a deep connection to every other contributor to the scheme, all the bodies meshed in the tangle with her, those above and below and to the side, but at the same time it couldn't truthfully be said that the animate mountain had a definite purpose. It was a gigantic flesh pyramid but a vastly indecisive one. When complete it would be a wanderer without a destination, lumbering first in one direction, then another, most likely returning to its starting point after a few hours. There was no central control to the thing. It was headless despite the numberless heads it contained within itself. Like a chaotic force of nature, pure cataclysm.

In other countries other pyramids would come together like this eventually. It was the first of its kind, this one, an experiment, a test. But one day the entire human race would form itself into a single truly enormous pyramid that would trundle over every continent and flatten ranges with its weight. Even oceans wouldn't be able to stop that behemoth. But this lay far in the future.

Months passed. Alex Carter turned up to make his observations when the pyramid was fully formed. He studied the site carefully with his binoculars before approaching and walking around it. He had a set of archaeology tools with him. He measured the height of the capstone with a theodolite.

An echo sounder revealed the existence of a chamber at the heart of the pulsating wonder. Then he selected an entry point.

Before he could begin digging his way into the side of the pyramid, some activity deep within the interior reached his ears. An object, a familiar presence, was moving towards him. He dropped the spade and used his hands to more gently push aside the sensual blocks. It was more like surgery than archaeology. What would his professors say if they could see him at work now?

Never before had the treasure inside a pyramid made efforts to escape on its own, to give itself to him, to save him at least some effort. A discovery like this could even establish his reputation as one of the greats. But no, he knew what was coming and it belonged only to itself. He stood back.

The pyramid disgorged a woman. Her hair was tangled and fell over her body like thick cords of rain, pouring over her distended belly, which she now held protectively with both hands. The pyramid began moving away behind her, setting off on another random ramble over the bare landscape.

She stepped closer and nodded at his unspoken question.

"I'm going to be a mummy!"

The Lighthouse Sisters

There are three sisters and I am fond of them all but only one of them is fond of me and I am not entirely sure which one that is. It might be the eldest and tallest but I only think this is so because she sometimes smiles at me and once twitched her nose charmingly at something I said.

It goes without saying that she has red hair and that this hair resembles fire and that when she walks through the rain I am astonished that no steam billows from the top of her head. She works in a shop and one day she was stringing up a chain of lightbulbs over the store front.

Oh look!
A long haired
ginger girl at the top of a
tall step ladder who
in a strong wind
shows no
fear.

But
it's surely
too late to resemble
the Pharos of Alexandria,
my dear?

Or is it too early…

That is the poem I wrote about her when I reached my apartment. It is true that she seems comfortable with heights and it was a very lofty step ladder. As for myself, I enjoy being at the apex of things, not metaphorically but literally and sometimes when I am leaning on my balcony I feel an impulse to shout the word "Fire!" and then jump into the void.

Summer is long over and autumn is more than halfway through and winter will be especially harsh this year, I can feel it. I am generally right about trivial things such as the weather and mostly wrong about existence, the universe and our purpose within it. Those three sisters!

The shop the eldest works in sells light fittings and lamps. At night all the bulbs are illuminated and then it seems the shop is a furnace and that the doors have been opened to allow the molten metal to pour out. But she emerges in her red shoes instead, carrying half the total glow with her on her head, her curls licking the air and crackling with energy.

There was a festive atmosphere in the city and she joined her friends in one of the squares. A strong young lad impudently offered her a ride on his back and she accepted. He marched around the square and down some of the adjacent streets and for a moment I thought there was a torchlight procession, perhaps an atavistic political event, taking place.

But no, it was just the eldest sister on the back of a stout fellow and he was growing tired and in fact he was ready to put her down, as a mythic hero of the distant past might also have felt weary after carrying a lighthouse, and I'm sure some hero did that, and she cautiously dismounted. There was no torchlight procession tonight. I had been mistaken.

This reminds me of something that once happened when I was walking in a park not far from my house. In the centre of the park is a circle of tall stones but it's not really ancient, it only looks like some important ritual site, and I thought someone had lit a blaze of branches there.

But it turned out to be a dog running in circles excitedly. From a distance it looked just like a fire and thoughts of druids and magic and sacrifices had filled me with alarm, but it was just a Red Setter, magnificently hairy, and I laughed at my foolishness, not because it was funny but to hear my own voice guffawing and enjoying itself. Good for it.

I decided to write another poem for this eldest sister.

Come
camping with
me tonight, O ginger girl,
for it will save
us both much time
and trouble.

There'll be no
need to light a fire
before bed,
we can just cook our
supper on your
head.

I think it is unlikely she will accept the invitation, even if I make her aware of it, which I have absolutely no intention of doing. One doesn't cook soup on a burning house, that's a well attested truth, and it would be equally uncouth to do so on a lighthouse flame, no matter how organic the structure, how female and willing it is. There are limits.

The second sister also has red hair but instead of resembling the fire of a famous classical lighthouse it seems, at least from behind, like the sail of a ship at sunset. It is straight rather than curly and presents an unbroken curtain to the view of one who happens to be following.

Not that I'm in the habit of following anyone deliberately! But let's be honest enough to admit that sometimes it does happen. You wish to go in the direction that best suits your needs, but the person ahead of you appears to want to go in the same direction. What can you do? Change direction and end up in a place you have no desire to be? Surely not.

I was standing at the end of a busy street one afternoon and wondering how I might make my way down it, so thickly thronged with pedestrians was it, when I noticed the gleam of the setting sun between the shoulders and heads of the milling crowd and I checked my wristwatch and said to myself, "That's too early!" but it wasn't the setting sun at all.

No, it was the hair of the middle sister, far away on her distant head at the other end of the street, but the sunset effect was incredibly strong. She is like an old-fashioned ship in other ways too, her nose a prow, her rump a rudder, her slow gestures like churning oars, her stockings like rigging, and she surges as she walks through fathomless modern life.

The third sister has short red hair like a rock slicked with blood. I imagine she has been used as a murder weapon, a bludgeon to smash the bones of a victim who probably deserved such a fate. How could I know any of this for certain? I am guessing, nothing more. These sisters fascinate me but I avoid the third one because she is geologically intimidating.

She looks up to the second sister, who looks up to the first sister, and this is the way it should be, but to see them standing together reminds me too much of a morbid bar chart, falling barometric pressure or the failure of the economy, the end of prosperity and decline of the west.

Do they have names, these sisters? You want to humanise them, take them away from the control of my definitions. Yes, they have names. Farina, Heeva, Recka, they are called. Unusual perhaps, but what is usual? There are too many usual things in the world that oppress and dominate people for me to have more than minimal respect for the conventional.

Farina intrigues me, the other two are not irrelevant, that's too harsh a way of putting it, but they are tangents on the curve of my understanding. Only the eldest daughter resembles a lighthouse and I want to bathe in the beams she throws off into the dark. But first I must provide the darkness! How can I do this? If I think sinister thoughts, will that be sufficient?

I have no desire to think thoughts in which I am unable to see, whether dark or foggy. And talking about fog reminds me that her laugh is exactly like a horn that roars over the swirly grey soup made from the condensing vapours that shroud the shore. Only a few times have I heard this laughter but it startled me on each occasion and made me convulse.

I ought to show her one of the many poems I have written for her. What do I have to lose? Only everything. But everything doesn't matter, because we are told that nothing is more important than love, and if nothing is so mighty that it takes precedence over everything, then nothing is the best outcome to aim for. That is logic. If I lose, I also gain.

You
are a freckled
girl and I'm a hale
and hearty
boy.

Kiss
me in my
vigorous prime and
taste a wine
divine.

I'll
lick your
freckles in return and
slurp a ginger
beer.

I am
the hale and
hearty boy who burned
his tongue last
year.

She won't be pleased by my words or the sentiments they express but there is the possibility she will be tolerant. That's more than enough for me. At least I can swear that my poems are heartfelt. I fold the page on which this verse exists into the shape of a boat and I leave it on the threshold of her shop like a beached vessel that went exploring for the lightest and brightest version of Atlantis, risen and dried out nicely, a dehydrated legend.

To my astonishment, the next time I'm passing her shop, more than a week later, she rushes out from the gaping doorway and seizes my wrists in her strong grip, swinging me around to face her twitching retroussé nose. She is taller than I am and I crane my neck to look up at her green eyes, but strands of angry red hair are covering them like streams of lava.

"Do you really believe I can be influenced by words?" she demands, and I am about to shake my head when she adds, "Well, to a certain small extent, yes I can. You will be given a chance," and when I quaveringly ask her to elucidate her tantalising meaning, she is more specific. "To amuse me, of course. Taking me out for a drink is your objective, no?"

It hadn't been until that very moment, but now it was, and so I nodded and she released my hands. The marks of her fingers remained on my flesh, slowly fading. What an unexpected development! Farina had always been an ideal for me rather than an individual it was possible to do things *with*. But to turn down a chance to be her companion for a few hours would be an unspecified sacrilege and I suggested a proper time and location.

"Very well, that will do," was her answer, and I went away like a man who has been informed that he must perform in a circus to entertain the clowns on a day when there are no paying audience members. The comparison is oblique but I was an oblique man at that moment, so it fits. I knew precisely which bar I was going to take her to, elegant and tranquil.

There is a superstition that I invented when I was younger, and despite the fact I'm aware it was manufactured by myself at a tender age in an idle moment, it has successfully incorporated itself into my belief system to the extent that it now seems very unwise to doubt its veracity.

It is the idea that everyone is allowed to cast a single spell in a lifetime, to make one wish. People either are unaware of this power and neglect to use it, or they waste their wish, using it to conjure up a minor delight that is forgotten in a few days. But I always kept my wish secure. I would finally employ it when I was with Farina and it would benefit both of us.

We met in the Lighthouse Bar on the seafront and I made sure I was early. She entered while I was watching the door and it seemed that a lamp had been lit and that the building could begin revolving. But it didn't do so. It was fixed on its foundations. We drank red wine and I said, "You are a lighthouse at heart and that is precisely why we are sitting here."

"I know almost nothing about the sea," she replied modestly, but this was a joke, for her very presence tugged at my soul and a tug is a thing of the sea, as anyone can affirm. On our third glass of wine I told her that this seaside town was no place for such a stupendous wonder as she was.

There was only one city in the world worthy to host her special form.

She wanted to know where that was and I told her. "Alexandria, the bride of the Mediterranean! Where else? That's where we should be right now, you and I, among the colonnades, white villas and wide boulevards of the greatest metropolis of ancient days. And I have one wish that I can use, untarnished and potent. Let me take us on a journey there!"

She laughed her foghorn laugh and all the wisps of doubt in my mind were shredded by its sonic magnificence. I told her about the Pharos, a tower that was almost a temple, and explained its dimensions and history, how it had served as the model for all lighthouses since, how its construction was ordered by one of the Ptolemies, taking twelve years to finish.

"One of the tallest man-made structures in the world of its time but that's a convenience of language only. You are a woman, an avatar of the Pharos, thrust into our own century for mysterious reasons. You blaze superbly but warn no ships of submerged reefs, yet I am sure you will serve as the model for every woman who will follow you. Even your sisters appreciate the deep truth of this and have done their best to imitate you."

She disagreed with me, that much was obvious, but I hadn't expected easy acquiescence on her part. It takes considerable time to convince someone that they are both a human being and a prominent structure of granite blocks topped with a platform on which shines a huge mirror during the day and where logs burn at night. Time or else a magical epiphany.

"I will use my solitary wish now. When we leave this bar we will be not in our modern town but in Alexandria as it was in its prime. Time and space are at my command. You will see and then no more persuasion will be necessary. Let me spend my wish on a blissful miracle!"

"In its prime," she echoed, but I had already closed my eyes, pressing my eyelids as firmly together as I could. I made my wish and when it was done and I opened my eyes, I was alarmed to note that she had gone. Had my talk worried her enough that she had fled while I wasn't looking? I finished my drink in one gulp, surprised it was a sweet liqueur and not the wine I had been drinking, and towards the door I hurriedly made my way.

If she had run out into the night, I would soon be on her heels. But the bar had changed dramatically during my prolonged blink. It was even more elegant than it had been, with chandeliers and softer lighting. How had the management altered the decor in such a short span of time? I lurched out into the street and I saw that in fact my wish had been granted.

The Lighthouse Bar had gone, vanished into the future, for I found myself in the past and I had just exited the Cecil Hotel. The sea lapped softly, a blue so dark it might as well be black, and the lights of the Corniche stretched along the slight curve of the bay. Yes, this was Alexandria! But there had been an error in my wish. I leaned on a palm tree for support.

Alexandria in its prime? I had assumed it would be classical times, the age of the Ptolemies and Cleopatra, the Great Library and Aristarchus, Eratosthenes, Hypatia, Ctesibius, and Hero, who invented a steam engine millennia before the Industrial Revolution. But no, the wish clearly had different ideas, other tastes, and it regarded the best days of the city to have been in the early 1930s, during the final chapter of British rule in Egypt.

Ah, the Cecil Hotel, where Somerset Maugham, Agatha Christie, Winston Churchill had often stayed! Where Umm Kulthum had performed her songs, the grandeur of empire's end, the slowly rotating ceiling fans and potted palms, the obscure liqueurs in bottles behind the bar!

I hurried to the edge of the Corniche, looking down at the narrow strip of sand washed by the incoming sea. Then I looked across to the end of the jutting headland where the Pharos had once stood. It was gone, of course, collapsed to rubble in a Fourteenth Century earthquake, its tumbled blocks recycled to form the ramparts of the Citadel of Qaitbay. The lighthouse had no role to play in this iteration of the prime time of Alexandria.

And this meant that Farina was vanished too, for she was an avatar of the structure and no avatar can survive the loss of its archetype for long. My wish had accidentally removed her from my life.

Should I write a new poem to express my melancholy appreciation of this irony? But I had no paper or pen with me. Then I noticed a ship on the sea and it was approaching the harbour. The moon had risen and it was blood red, as if pretending to be the setting sun, and its light stained the sails of the vessel. The second daughter, Heeva, was sailing into port! Could it be that she was the one who was fond of me after all? How strange!

But without a working lighthouse to warn her, the ship had no chance with the deadly rocks that make Alexandria such a hazardous place for navigation. I saw how the waves lapped against a large round rock directly in the path of the hull and I realised that this was the third sister. Recka was waiting to smash the timbers of Heeva. So it was the third sister who was secretly fond of me too? I was indirectly responsible for this chaos.

Sibling rivalry taken to extremes! Recka couldn't bear losing me to Heeva and planned to sabotage her sister's efforts to reach me. Or was I deluded? Did these events really have nothing to do with my existence? In old cartoons there is a convention that an inspired idea can be represented by a spherical lightbulb coming on over one's head. My sudden insight was that I was superfluous to all that was happening, that I too was a wreck.

In anguish I began to turn on my heel, throwing out wide beams from the imaginary bulb that crowned my cranium.

Three sisters
    and one is a lighthouse,
    one a ship,
    the other a rock,
        and I am just a man
        out of time with the world
        who has had an idea
            that illuminates his own place
            but also reaches out
        across the perilous sea.

Toot and Come In

It was raining heavily and the raindrops tasted like river water on her tongue. A good sign or an ill omen? Róta wasn't sure. Nor did she even know what might be the difference between them. She waited. At last a car turned the corner and she extended her arm. The raindrops bouncing on the road generated thick mist and the headlamps of the vehicle prodded the vapour like parallel spears or two beams in the roof of a drinking hall.

Róta nodded her appreciation of this effect, her hair streaming. The driver saw her and stopped the car. She opened the back door, settled into the seat and slammed the door shut against the storm. The driver spoke without turning his head. His voice was gruff and weary.

"Where to, lady?"

"Start the meter and keep driving. I'll tell you which way to go. It's much too difficult to explain. I'm late."

"I don't have a meter. None of us do these days. Those times have gone. I need to know your destination."

"Just drive and I'll pay you. Believe me, you won't regret it. Five pounds for every minute of the journey."

"That's a lot, lady."

"Take it or leave it. But drive fast."

"In this chaos, I can only go a moderate speed safely," he said, but his foot pressed on the accelerator. They moved out into the frenzied darkness. Although the wind had dropped, the cloudburst continued unabated. The road was turning into a stream, with the sort of rapids that a brave canoeist would love to shoot, a churning of froth and dark foam.

Róta said, "Turn left at the next junction."

The driver said, "Sure."

She was aware that he was observing her in the mirror, and so she glared at him in turn, her eyes cold, piercing, a dark blue almost black. There was nothing predatory in his own gaze, simply a curiosity too worn out to be anxiety or fear. Yet his reason was disturbed, even if his emotions remained bland. Róta had the overbearing presence of a prize fighter.

"Lady," he said, strategically, "my name is Carter."

"Take the next right."

He did so, and then he joked. "Take the next right? It's the government that keeps taking our rights. One by one."

"Yours, perhaps," responded Róta, "but not mine."

"Well, that's nice."

"Just keep driving. Left again here."

"Lady, I was an archaeologist. I'm educated. I know things. Driving a taxi for a living isn't my dream."

"Forget about such things as dreams."

He rubbed his brow.

"I get some in the back who love to talk, won't stop talking. Others remain silent the whole way. Then there are those like you, enigmatic, I guess, baffling and alluring, but not endearing."

"Mr Carter, we are approaching a roundabout."

"Correct. Which exit?"

"No exit. Keep circling and don't stop."

"Are you serious?"

"Yes, always. I'm a daughter of destiny."

"Can't argue with that."

But his implication was that he didn't understand her, couldn't imagine any plausible motive for the way she spoke. He wondered if she was insane, high on drugs, playing a contemptible prank. He deserved her coldness for his attempt to flirt with her, calling her alluring.

That had been a mistake and he hadn't even meant to say it. He reached the roundabout and made two complete revolutions before remarking, "It will make us dizzy if we keep doing this."

"No, it won't. And I meant what I said."

"Five pounds per minute?"

"That's right. The vortex is necessary."

"That's a new one."

"The vortex is as old as the elder gods."

"The quip, I meant."

He shuddered for the first time, a slow spasm that began at the base of his spine and ended at the nape of his neck. Róta stared out of the window, clouded with smeared raindrops, pressing her face hard into the glass. The turning was working, the landscape was changing, melting and flowing. The colours of the sky were shifting along the spectrum. The drab tones of grey had evolved into a selection of dark oranges and vermilions. The circumference of the roundabout was expanding, rapidly and smoothly.

The curvature became less extreme, the steering was easier. The tension in the driver's muscles gradually lessened. Róta was glad he was durable. He was adequate for her purposes and she felt softer towards him, less contemptuous of his naïve questions and apprehension.

The sensation of turning in a circle was no longer apparent. The radius of the roundabout was now so long that she felt they were driving along a perfectly straight highway. The driver cried:

"What happened? What is happening now?"

"Keep going," she said.

Róta smiled to herself, but she was uneasy. Her mind examined the recent events that had led to her sitting in the back of a taxi. An accident in the sky, an unprecedented incident in her long life.

She was supposed to be able to dodge the lightning bolts with the greatest of ease, just as her sisters did. But that electric strike had darted sidewise at her, the tongue of a fire serpent, enveloping her in a dark turquoise shimmer, just as the mutating landscape outside the taxi windows was pulsing with a blue-green radiance of its own making. But what if it hadn't been a bolt of lightning? She considered the implications of this possibility. A meteorite? Another being, also winged, also on a supernatural mission?

Perhaps a rocket, deliberately launched at her. An anti-aircraft missile from a hostile military force. It didn't bear thinking about. She was the one in charge when it came to combat situations.

The taxi was accelerating. They were heading towards a star that rose over an impossible distant horizon. This star was like a gem, twinkling, beckoning, a transparent crucible filled with red and green lava. One of her favourite stars but of minimal use in her everyday existence.

"Lady, I'm bewildered."

"The roundabout has ceased to exist, that's all."

"Is this a kind of magic?"

"Drive straight ahead. Focus on your task. Don't stop, don't allow yourself to be distracted by anything you might see on either side. The road is safe, it is a stable bridge across the dimensions."

"Five pounds for every minute! I'll concentrate on that."

He was shivering again.

The fear would pass. It was nothing more than unfamiliarity with the act of crossing between worlds. Róta almost sympathised with him, not quite, it would have been against her vows. She controlled herself. She no longer disdained him and that was a significant mood swing. She decided to explain, to put him out of his misery or perhaps increase it.

"We are travelling through time as well as space. This is a shortcut. But the road is often hazardous. My sacred calling compels me to travel to a destination that is remote chronologically."

"Sacred? You mean you are a nun?"

Róta smirked. "Mr Carter, there is little to be gained in conversation at this juncture. Your existence hasn't prepared you for the truth. I have said more than enough already. Please desist."

"But I *was* an archaeologist. I *am* educated."

She frowned and said:

"What civilisations have you dug deep into?"

"All over, everywhere."

"I value precision, Mr Carter."

"Mesopotamia. The Indus Valley. I was in Brazil for two years, looking for lost cities in the forest, on the banks of tributaries of the Amazon. I was in Peru too. Polynesia. I even found Viking artefacts on the Azores! They reached those islands before anyone else—"

"You know much about Norse culture?"

"I believe I do, yes."

"Mr Carter, I am a *valkyrie*, one of the choosers of the slain. I fly to collect the souls of warriors who die in battle. There are many of us. We fill the sky like clouds of arrows, we dart here and there, not only above the inhabited regions of the world but over the oceans."

"I see, you are one of those winged women."

"My name is Róta."

The driver was nodding and with each nod his anxiety weakened. He was too enthralled to be terrified now.

He spoke slowly, reverently. "You are mentioned in a chapter of the book *Gylfaginning*. I have read it. I have imagined you. Your name is connected with sleet and powerful storms."

"That is very erudite of you, Mr Carter."

She leaned forward and touched him lightly on the shoulder. He squirmed but her praise had strengthened him.

"Lady, I never wanted to be a taxi driver, it's just the way things happened, my dreams were dashed by circumstances. I could have been a bigshot, perhaps a museum director, who knows?"

"Your time has not yet come," she answered.

He sighed at this ambiguity. "I am nervous of time, damned nervous. But why a taxi?" he wanted to know.

"An emergency. I was flying, responding to a call. A mighty warrior fated to die in battle, his head split into two pieces by a curved blade. His soul will be perfect for Valhalla. I will take him there. He will be welcomed as an *einherjar*, a new recruit who must practise fighting and killing and dying again and again, cut to pieces every day, reformed every night until *Ragnarök*, the end of worlds and time and everything else. But you know all that, I'm sure, Mr Carter. I was blasted out of the sky. I fell."

"You mean that you injured yourself?"

"My wings are shrivelled."

"But they'll regrow, won't they? You're a supernatural being. You can also be reformed, like the warriors."

"I don't know. Shrivelled *and* charred."

"Charred is pretty bad."

"Mr Carter, this is why I need you to drive me. You know of the culture to which I belong. You have excavated longships from the mud of river estuaries, found swords and coins in burial mounds. That's all well and good. But we are going far away from Viking lands. The warrior whose soul I am going to collect has never heard of Odin or Thor. He lived and died in a desert land bisected by a great river with pyramids shining at noon, white limestone blinding the eyes, a realm of crocodile gods and jackals."

"Egypt, yes I know about it. I know Egypt."

"I am going for a soul."

"You collect the souls of warriors who believe in other deities? Lady, that really does amaze me. It seems—"

"They are needed. Everyone is needed."

"For the final battle?"

She touched his shoulder again and then pointed ahead and he squinted at the gem on the horizon. "That star," she said, "is Sirius. It has risen and the Nile will flood. We must arrive before the banks overflow. We *will* arrive in time. It is impossible for us to ever be late."

Before he could respond to this, she added, "I like the way you drive, I am impressed by your self-control."

"Lady, the most important control is over my vehicle. There are shapes on the verges of this road. I don't appreciate them very much. What are they? They appear to be trying to hitch a ride."

"Ignore them, for your own sake and mine. They are wisps, genies, devils, seducers, ghouls and wraiths."

He nodded. His hands were firm on the steering wheel.

"Take the next offramp."

"Offramp, lady? I don't see one."

"That slip road. There it is. Slow down, slide onto it. Egypt can be found in that direction, Ancient Egypt."

He steered the car off the main highway, out of the chronoflow, back into a relatively stable and slow-moving present, a contemporary past, once distant to him but not vital and immediate.

"Lady, is this really Egypt as it once was?"

"No, Mr Carter, it is the land of the pharaohs as it is *now*. I am here to pick up the soul of Thutmose the Third, one of the greatest warriors of the history of the nation. He was killed in battle but the archaeologists, as I'm sure you know, say that his mummy was damaged by tomb robbers shortly after his burial. No, he was mortally wounded in combat."

"Lady, that is a valuable insight."

"He was the guiding star of the Eighteenth Dynasty and I am here to guide him to Valhalla and introduce him to gods he never suspected existed. See that building emerging from the shimmer of the sun on the desert sands? His palace. Drop me off near the entrance."

"Is that all, lady?"

"Wait outside. Do you understand?"

"Your instructions are clear. I am also clear on the point of five pounds per minute. It's entirely worthwhile."

She nodded, but her mouth was unsmiling. The palace loomed out at them from the heatwave and the dust. He changed to a lower gear, braked, waited for her to get out of the car. She went into the palace, moving rapidly, lithe, lethal, a terrible but enchanting figure.

He kept the engine ticking over, ready for a quick getaway, but a getaway to where? Without her help, he was hopeless, lost in a well of time, the depths of the ages, and his old instincts were aroused now, his curiosity about the past and his love of what was long gone. The ruins of the human race, the lesson the eroded remains still had to teach.

She returned before he had stopped daydreaming.

"I've made a mistake!"

She was distraught, baffled, her hands clenched into fists that could punch stone into crumbs. He braced himself. She said, "My accident must have done more than destroy my wings. It seems to have impaired my brain too. I made a navigational error. Yes, this is Egypt in the Eighteenth Dynasty, but we have arrived eighty years too late."

"Thutmose isn't there? Who is there, lady?"

"A snivelling boy king."

He knew immediately whom she was referring to.

"What will you do now?"

"I'll take him anyway, Mr Carter. He won't be much use in Valhalla. But I can't return empty handed. He's a weakling and Odin will be annoyed with me but I am pressed for time. Already I am being called to another destination. The moment of truth has arrived."

"What truth? What's truth anyway?"

"I have no wings. I need transport. I am going to offer you a job. I want an official chauffeur. I want you in that role. It's the only solution that makes sense in the circumstances. Well?"

He accepted without hesitation.

She said, "Five pounds a minute. That's a lot of pounds. The boy king is a slip of a thing. I'll have to kill some of his eunuchs too. Five pounds of flesh for every minute that you drove me."

To her relief, he didn't recoil at this revelation. He had expected some sort of twist all along. He was ready.

"I'm going back into the palace, Mr Carter. I suggest you drive around the building once. Just to be certain there are no other *valkyries* on the other side who might be spying on me. I will be ready when you return. The weak pharaoh and his guards are doomed."

"Who is this king? Tell me his name."

"Ask another question. I'll answer both with one reply."

"What will I do when I'm back here?"

"Toot and come in."

They looked at each other, driver and supernatural woman, and then with a sound as wild as that of a sandstorm, they laughed. Róta hurried into the palace and he released the handbrake, still chuckling, tears of awful mirth rolling down his cheeks to his pyramidal chin.

Cloud Hunter

I am a cloud hunter. I have returned from my latest mission and it was a failure and now I am anxious about how the pharaoh will receive my news. I am sure he will punish me. How severe will he be? I might be exiled or worse, my boat confiscated, my reputation in tatters.

You tell me not to worry, to be reassured. You say there is an old proverb for one in my predicament. "The mouth of a man saves him," you declare, and you advise me to entertain the pharaoh with the drama of my mission, turning it from a failure into an amusing story.

Something similar happened to you once. That is why you feel confident I will be spared humiliation. You were also a cloud hunter. You were the captain of a ship bigger than mine, big enough for a crew of one hundred sky sailors. It is an impressive number, certainly. Those were the days when huge clouds still thronged the skies, clouds larger than pyramids, five or ten times the size of the tiddlers we must be satisfied with now.

You have embarked on your narrative in the same way I embarked on my mission, with a clear objective but no way of knowing for sure you will attain it successfully. But my ears are open, I am listening. I am not the kind of man to get up in the middle of a story and stamp off, sneering at the wisdom of elderly people. I am full of admiration for you.

And so you set off in your ship, ascending rapidly in a tight helix, singing as you rose. You were a young skipper but experienced enough and yet as your vessel climbed higher and higher it encountered clear air turbulence and shook like a landed fish. This was nothing unusual. The sailors were strapped to their benches and they gripped the oars hard.

Then a sandstorm arose and the particles of sand reduced visibility almost to zero. It seemed to come from nowhere and rocked the ship more violently, a storm the likes of which you had never encountered before. As your vessel took a plunge, your men tightened their grips until their knuckles whitened. But you were standing at the prow, leaning against the wooden rail, and this awful lurch tipped you overboard. Down you plunged.

That should have been your doom. A man might survive falling into a sea or river, but sky sailors have no such hope. Your body would be shattered when it made contact with the ground. And yet, you say, that was not the outcome of your accident. You plummeted only a trivial distance before crashing through a palm tree's fronds and landing, essentially uninjured, on soft alluvial soil. Then you blinked and stood up and gazed around.

You found yourself on an island, an island in the sky.

Well, that is possible, I suppose.

Sky boats fly. There is no reason why an island shouldn't. Indeed, what if a sky boat was abandoned by its crew? It might remain aloft, gathering dust, sand particles, seeds blown thither from the trees and flowers of distant forests, grime and soot from fires below, and slowly grow in size, completely covering the hull of the boat, which may well have rotted to nothing beneath. I believe that such a levitating landmass is feasible, old man.

And so you lived alone on that island, enjoying spectacular views when the storm dissipated. You ate the dates and figs provided by an unnatural Nature. As the island floated towards the ocean and back, moving at random in the sky, you were able to quench your thirst by sipping the condensation of mist and fog that trickled down the trunks of the trees.

But still you did not neglect your spiritual duties.

You prayed to the gods often.

And one afternoon, several months after you had arrived on the island, you succeeded in making a fire and dedicating it to Sekhmet and Ptah, roasting some dates as a sacrificial offering, the best you could do under the circumstances. No man might have been able to do more.

Then the ground shook and the head of a gigantic serpent pushed itself out of the moist soil and the head of this monster opened and asked you, "Who was the person who brought you to the island?" Unable to answer, because no single individual was responsible for the accident, you merely shrugged. But the snake repeated the question two more times.

Why the serpent was so keen to know the answer is still a mystery to you. I agree that it seems unimportant. The snake invited you to his home, in a cavern under the surface of the soil, and you deemed it wiser not to refuse. In that cool space, the serpent asked you the same question three more times, and you were finally compelled to respond properly.

You told the snake, "Ultimately it was the pharaoh who brought me to this island, because he has ordered men to sail in boats into the sky and hunt clouds and bring them to him in his palace."

The serpent laughed at you, not unkindly, and asked you not to fear. It was not the pharaoh who had brought him to the island but destiny itself. That is the answer that is always true. "You will be rescued before too long," continued the snake, "but now permit me to tell a story of my own. Stories are the only things I have of value here, and because my tongue is forked I can tell two at the same time, or just one at twice the speed."

The serpent then related how he had lived on the island with his family in a tribe that contained almost one hundred members. But a star fell from the night, a meteorite, and landed in the middle of the island, punching a hole through it, a hole that now served as a cloud trap.

Yes, it was true, the clouds floated through the hole but were too wide and ended up stuck there. The impact sent shockwaves through the flying island and killed all the snakes apart from himself. He had been lonely since that moment. He had been waiting for a visitor and now the marooned sky sailor was a guest of his household.

"I will tell you all I know, all the secrets of the snake species, and in return you will tell me tales."

That was the arrangement. You swapped stories. The serpent didn't really want anything else from you, and this was a relief, for you had supposed at first that it would swallow you whole. You made a promise to the snake that if you were rescued, you would inform the pharaoh of the excellence of his serpentine generosity, and the snake assured you again that you certainly would be found and taken home, and he told you more secrets, incredible secrets, how to twist your body into a knot, for example.

And so it happened that one day, a passing sky boat spotted you and threw you a line and you swung across, and you were so excited to be rescued that it seemed unimportant that the island had a hole in it that was a cloud trap. After you had reported your discovery to the pharaoh, he would surely send out new boats, perhaps in fleets, to find it and tow it down to the ground on grapples. A thousand clouds would water our parched land and help to keep the desert away for a few more generations at least.

That was your reasoning. And the pharaoh was pleased with your tale and you were not regarded as a failure. So you say the same to me. I will also not be regarded as a failure if I make the account of my fruitless mission entertaining. I must turn it into an amusing story.

That is all very well, old man, and I appreciate your attempts at reassuring me. But the mission I was sent on was the finding of your sky island. My orders were to bring it back with its cloud trap full of clouds. We located the island by pure chance. We sailed towards it.

My oarsmen were overwhelmed by the sight. They were unable to operate as skilfully as usual. We sailed into the cloud trap, right through it in fact. As we did so, we dislodged all the clouds trapped there, freeing them. They fled as fast as they could towards the horizon, vanishing over it, leaving our desert behind. The disturbance in the air that our ship made as it passed through the hole in the middle of the island, tipped the island over and it crashed down on the ground, breaking into fragments with the impact.

This is an entertaining narrative, no doubt, but do you really think that if I tell it to the pharaoh, he will regard it as equivalent to all that lost water? I fear that your magical snake was also killed.

You have given me wise advice but I believe it is worthless. "The mouth of a man saves him." Not in my case. It will condemn me. As I said before, I am a cloud hunter. I have returned from my latest mission. It was a failure. Now I am anxious about how the pharaoh will receive my news. He will punish me. How severely? This is what concerns me.

What was that? He already knows what happened and has passed sentence on me? How is that possible? The serpent survived, slithered to his palace, told him everything. I am being punished right now. Not exile or confiscation of my property. Nothing to do with my reputation. You have been assigned to me. You are going to tell me stories forever?

For the rest of my life, your tales, your wise advice!

And now you are coiling yourself around me, holding me tight, so that it's impossible for me to get away. The snake taught you how to do that. You have learned his lessons well. And next?

The same story again? And then again and again!

I am your prisoner, a listener.

You tell me not to worry, to be reassured. You say there is an old proverb for a man in my predicament. But I am a cloud hunter. I have returned from my latest mission and it was a failure.

The Taming of the Old Woman Who Lived in a Shrew

When King Zoser is tired of finding sand in his bread, he calls for beer. When he is tired of finding sand in his beer, he calls for bread. He knows he is happy because the year is turning as it should.

"What I need," he decides, "is what I already have."

Through the narrow windows of his palace, he watches the flooding of the Nile. He sees copper swords bent into sickles on the forge of the knee, the reaping of the tall grasses, the sickles bent back into swords.

At other times, while priests burn offerings on stone altars, he plays board games in the gloom. Or else he lounges with his wife, counting the spiders that twirl their webs on the cracked plaster of the lofty ceiling.

"What I do not need," he decides, "is what I do not have."

One bright morning, listening to the reed pipes of musicians, and covering his gaping yawn with a heavily-ringed hand, his repose is shattered by the arrival of a messenger who, glistening with sweat and gasping for breath, crashes through the solid air of the palace. "A message, O King!" The fellow casts himself at the foot of the dais on which rests the throne.

"Yes?" King Zoser waves a languid hand.

Prostrate before his mighty ruler, the messenger merely trembles and clutches at the cool stone. King Zoser sighs.

"A message you say? What message?"

The fellow clambers to his feet, brushes himself down and holds aloft a piece of papyrus. He squints in the light and frowns. "A giant shrew has invaded the land and is eating all the grain in the granaries."

King Zoser stands up and tugs at his beard. "This is serious!" He takes a couple of steps down from his throne and pauses. "Are you *sure* a giant mouse has invaded our land and is eating the grain in the granaries?"

The messenger fumbles with the message. "Not a mouse. A shrew."

"Where has this mouse come from?"

"A shrew, my lord."

King Zoser strides up to the fellow, snatching the papyrus away and bearing it to a smoky oil lamp that gutters in a recess in the wall. He scratches his head. "What does this bit say?" he demands, pointing.

The messenger timidly peers over his shoulder. "Giant shrew."

"And what about that bit?"

"Has invaded the land," says the messenger.

King Zoser scowls. It is a magnificent scowl, one of his best, and from a man who is no novice in the art. "I can read the rest for myself." He dismisses the messenger with a wave. The messenger retreats back the way he has come, bowing and scraping his forehead on the floor. King Zoser crumples up the message and mutters the dread words, "Eating the grain in the granaries."

There is silence in the room. Then he claps his hands.

"Summon my priests and priestesses, my astronomers and astrologers, my mystics and soothsayers, my sorcerers and philosophers, my wise men and wiser women, my chiromancers and necromancers, my readers of entrails, clouds and dreams, my best advisors and ministers. Summon them all!"

Gongs sound. Copper trumpets blare. From all corners of the palace, holy men and scholars and viziers and other diverse worthies come running. King Zoser now remounts the steps to his throne and waits for them to gather before him. It is a long wait. Some of the priests are so old that they have to be roused from their death beds to attend their master's call. Eventually, when the hall is crammed nearly full, King Zoser makes his announcement:

"A giant mouse has invaded our land and is raiding all our granaries. Something must be done about it. But what?"

There is a concerned muttering among the assembly. This muttering, King Zoser knows, will go on forever if he doesn't put a stop to it. He stamps his foot and silence falls like an overripe pomegranate on the head of a sleeping eunuch.

"Well?" he demands.

"Well what?" comes the unanimous reply.

King Zoser points at one of the figures in the crowd, a very aged and respected minister. "You there! Tell me what is to be done." He motions for the minister to step forward. "What do you think?" The minister bows deeply, joints a-creak, and opens his mouth. His jaw works silently, his teeth like burnt umber.

"What was that?" King Zoser cups his hand around his ear. "Speak up man! I can't hear a word you're saying."

Another figure steps forward. "Forgive him sire. He is so old and his voice has grown so faint that no one has been able to understand anything he has said for the last twenty years."

"Who are you and what advice do you have to offer?"

"I am Neskhons, your high Priestess, keeper of the keys of Amon, caresser of the thighs of Horus, nibbler of the lobes of..."

"Yes, yes! But what do you think?"

"I am not paid to think, lord. I am paid merely to intone endlessly and sway from side to side while acolytes oil my naked body and..."

"Not relevant." King Zoser mops his damp forehead. He points to another fellow. "You there! You are an astrologer, by the look of you. What do you think should be done about this giant mouse?"

"Giant mouse?" The astrologer blinks surprised eyes.

"Yes by Thoth! A giant mouse!"

"Ah!" The astrologer searches his memory and finally finds what he seeks. "It has never happened before. Therefore it can't be happening now."

King Zoser considers this gem. "Do you not think that such a view is just a little too conservative?"

The astrologer beams. "Thank you, lord."

King Zoser throws up his hands in despair. "Dismiss them all!" he wails. "All of them!" Instantly gongs sound and copper trumpets blare. The diverse worthies depart as asthmatically as they came, some of the aged priests making it back to their death beds with not a second to spare. King Zoser frets and paces and clutches his royal forehead and kicks the divine cat and lets loose a single tear.

He is comforted by a sultry hand, as sure and stable as the Nile itself (father of plane geometry, ribbon of the world) which descends on his shoulder as lightly as the ambitions of a bat. King Zoser turns round, glum and pained, but he cannot help but smile when he sees the owner of the hand and the eyes that are more mirthful than any smile.

"Ah, dear heart, how my own heart aches! This morning there was order to the world, everything was in its place, but now the cosmos is a terrible thing indeed, a thing of gigantic fluctuations, a reality where giant hungry mice can cross our borders unmolested!"

"A shrew, my lord." The voice is warm and soft, but very cunning. And King Zoser nods sombrely and knows again why this one is his principal wife and not some lowly concubine.

"You have an idea, my cool sherbet, I can tell."

"Yes, I have an idea."

"As always. It is you who run this realm, fluffy-tuft, and not I. Well, I am resigned and I am no fool. What's this idea of yours? And how much will it cost the treasury?"

Long lashes blink and dimples genuflect. King Zoser melts instantly, as he never fails to do. And the lovely pink mouth opens and a whisper escapes, waving its arms and chuckling silently in a restrained celebration of an unexpected freedom.

"I know someone who may be able to help. Do you remember that fellow known as Imhotep? The odd one with the peculiar habits?"

"Imhotep? It rings a copper bell, my jug of fig wine; a very battered copper bell. One without the clapper, probably. Was he the geographer who insisted that there lay lands beyond the desert which were inhabited by monsters and dwarves and three-eyed men?"

"No, my lord. That was cousin Hetepsekhemui. Imhotep was the one who called himself an 'architect'. He came to you last year with a design for a pyramid."

King Zoser snaps his fingers. "Of course, my gorgeous wading bird, I remember now! These pyramids of his were colossal affairs that would never fall down because they were in the shape of a building that has already fallen down. A pyramid shape no less! But how could he possibly help us? Last time he was here, I showed him the door."

"A very fine door as well, my lord, of that I have no doubt. But I think I detected the germ of a real idea in his work. I believe that we could use his services to our benefit this time."

"How so, my delectable dung beetle?"

"Perhaps we could commission him to design a special sort of building for us. The sort of building that has never been built before."

"Never been built before? What sort of building has never been built before? That is an impossible thought!"

"A giant mousetrap, lord."

King Zoser steps back a pace. His fingers worry the lines of astonishment that crowd around his eyes. He is the centre of this land, the centre of the universe, and wherever he moves this centre moves with him. But here, standing before him, is the true hub of all. She moves in the shadows like the dream within a dream he once had, long ago.

"A giant mousetrap, eh? What a capital idea! Summon him at once, my cool horizon, my weaver of wonders!"

"I have already made inquiries, my lord. It appears that he is on holiday at this present time."

"On holiday? But where?"

"Egypt of course. Where else is there?"

"Ah you tease me, little copper jar. Send messengers, I implore you. We must have this mousetrap at all costs."

She bows a deep bow, a curve like the spine of a harp, and departs into the shadows. Everywhere there are shadows. The filtered sunlight makes fine pearls of the dust of long ages; dust engendered from the trickles of purple sand that somehow always find their way in, and from the clippings of the beards of long-dead Kings, the desiccated skins of asps and toads.

King Zoser is tired of this twilight. He takes himself and his crown down one of the adjoining passages and up a flight of clay steps to a short balcony overlooking the river (bringer of the fertile clays of Kush, thread in the needle of Isis) which winks and glares far below. Sacred crocodiles snap and shower among the reeds. Boats ply the aeons.

And King Zoser is suddenly aware of the massive responsibility that has descended upon him. He feels his oldest ancestors calling out to him from their tombs beyond the fertile lands, lost tombs that have sunk beneath rolling dunes as large as cities. They cry: the cause of stability lies on your shoulders, if you fail yourself, you also fail the world.

And King Zoser makes many a shudder in the hot day, and in the shimmer and haze of the distant desert he thinks that he perceives a host come to meet him. A host of all his forebears. King Narmer, first of the Pharaohs, who united the two kingdoms and ended the strife between the followers of Horus and Set; Menes, the digger of canals, son of lithe Nithotep, who moved the capital from Hieraconpolis to Memphis; sombre Qaa, of whom records tell little; stern Khasekhemui, vanquisher of Libyans and sundry nomads. They file in procession towards him, angry and stately and very dead and King Zoser turns away and hides his face.

He descends back to the throne room. A new messenger is awaiting him, face as pale as a low moon. He eyes the fellow harshly. "What now?"

"A message, O King!" The messenger's words warble as his lips tremble. "The giant mouse is not a real mouse at all! It seems that a door opened in its belly at noon and let out a woman who spoke our tongue with a strange accent. This woman is the fruit in the mouse's cheeks, and the ripe fruits in her own cheeks are words of dire peril!"

"Shrew," corrects King Zoser. "Not a mouse. A shrew."

The messenger nods. "As you say, lord. But this was at Saqqara. Your general, Sinuhe, saw all. He conversed with this woman. She said terrible things in a silly voice. She claimed to be a 'Sybil'."

"Sybil who?" King Zoser grows alarmed. He thinks better of allowing the messenger to reply. He tears the papyrus from his hands and attempts to devour its full meaning himself. He shakes his dour head and frightens the messenger with a fierce look. He is convinced now that the gods are mocking him: dog-faced Anubis and mysterious Ptah and bundle-of-laughs Osiris, who is King of the dead as surely as he, Zoser, is King of the living, a much harder task.

One word he keeps repeating to himself, "No."

The messenger merely bows, as if this exclamation is a command; and he tries to follow this bow with thoughts of negation. He has taken King Zoser's denial as a denial of everything and he is willing to comply. There is no desert, no sky, no fingers on earthy Geb; no horizon of the sun, no lines around the blaze-bright mouth of Ra, and these are the pearls that were his eyes no more, and there are no teeth to pierce the crocodile tongue of Sobek or desert breeze to ruffle the ostrich feather on the head of Maat, and Bes is a dwarf no longer.

"Depart!" King Zoser is hoarse, but the messenger retreats and there is at least some stability in the fact that the King is troubled as before and holds his face in his bejewelled hands again.

The shadow of a lean reed of a man falls long on the shifting floor. King Zoser looks up to confront this latest arrival. Behind him stands a more familiar reed, his best beloved wife, like a puppeteer who dangles idiots on strings and sticks. The shadow folds in half.

"Your majesty! I am Imhotep, whom you have summoned. I have heard of your worries, my lord. I am the balm for your burns."

"Ah yes, Imhotep! The strange one? Events are moving too rapidly for one who measures his minutes as years. Not only has our land been invaded by a giant mouse, but this mouse speaks with the voice of a hag! An old woman emerges from its belly and makes cryptic remarks!" He waves the papyrus and fans the beads of moisture on his brow. "According to this report, we have a 'Sybil' who claims that the giant mouse is a 'time machine' created by an inventor who calls himself 'Daedalus'. She has come from a land that lies in the future, a mighty power named 'Greece' that exists when Egypt is falling mainly into the dust. What can this mean? Why does she claim to be stealing grain for her own people?"

"Why indeed, lord? She is obviously a madwoman, touched by the sun, who can prate only nonsense. There is no land called 'Greece' and there never will be. There is only Egypt."

King Zoser laughs bitterly. "Yet there is something here which makes me tremble more than any bad dream. This 'Daedalus' seems a mighty inventor. He has created a flying machine and a labyrinth from which no man can escape and now he wishes to provide grain to feed the armies of his people, who are besieging a city called 'Troy'. All this was faithfully reported to me by one of my most honest generals, Sinuhe of the withered arm and rheumy eye."

"I do not believe this, your majesty. But at any rate, I am a greater inventor than this 'Daedalus'. I have already designed the mousetrap that your majesty requires. Possibly you would care to see the plans?"

Cool frown, a finger-stroke along the temples of the divine head. King Zoser's temples are where offerings of his own blood boil and steam their smokes up to the heaven of the palace roof.

One word he keeps repeating to himself, "Yes."

Imhotep steps forward and offers his own piece of papyrus to his King, who takes it and glares. Insanity of insanities, sayeth the preacher, all is insanity. King Zoser slaps the design. "What is this?"

"A mousetrap, my lord. A trap to catch a mouse."

"No. It is a pyramid."

Imhotep shuffles uneasily on his axis. "Yes, I do admit that it bears a superficial resemblance. But it is, I can assure you, a giant mousetrap."

"It is four badly drawn triangles. It is another pyramid. You are trying to deceive me. I don't see how a giant mouse could be trapped by such an object, unless it were hollow and lowered down onto the mouse. An impossible feat."

"I agree. Therefore it is not hollow. It is solid stone all the way through. A superb structure, if I may say so. One that will speak out to generations to come of the glory of Imhotep... I mean, the glory of King Zoser. And it will be climbed by dozens for a magnificent view of the desert and possibly other pyramids which could also be built nearby."

"I think not."

Aware of his slip of the tongue, Imhotep gnashes his teeth, like flint against flint. King Zoser can almost smell the sparks.

"It might be a good idea if you were to depart from my sight and not return until you have prepared a sensible design for a mousetrap," King Zoser says, in a voice as sharp as a copper chisel. Imhotep lingers for an undecided moment and then turns on his heel and flees with a long moan, his arms waving in the air.

"That was unwise." His principal wife shakes her noble head and strokes his arm. "You did not give him a chance."

"He didn't deserve one." King Zoser is stubborn. There is now a great shout from without. "What next?" he wails. "Have I not suffered enough?" He looks up at heaven and then down again at the weary world. The shout grows louder and there is an edge of hysteria to it. But at the same time it is more than a little tinged with relief.

A figure as squat as Imhotep was lean drags itself towards the mighty ruler and throws itself on the floor, like the stub of a dice-stick from a worn cloth bag. The figure keeps tight hold on broken spear and warped shield and it is the copper helmet alone that rolls and clatters to a standstill at the base of the throne as the figure strikes its forehead in supplication upon the stones. "Hail!"

"And who might you be?" King Zoser chews his lip in anguish.

"Sinuhe, my lord! Your most loyal and dedicated general. Slayer of the nomads of the north and suppressor of the emergent kingdoms of the south. Sinuhe who lately has battled with a mystic shrew..."

"Aha! Sinuhe of the withered arm and rheumy eye?"

"No longer, my lord. They have got better. I am now Sinuhe of the warty nose and perforated ear."

"No wonder I didn't recognise you! But what are you doing here in my palace? You are supposed to be battling the giant mouse and the harridan who is its malign occupant. Are you completely defeated?"

"Quite the opposite, my lord. The shrew has been destroyed and its aged pilot well and truly tamed. An earthquake struck during the battle and both fell down a crevice that opened in the belly of the world. The mouse and the Sybil are no more!"

"An earthquake! But I felt nothing!"

"It was a very small earthquake, lord." Noticing King Zoser's disbelieving expression, Sinuhe clears his throat. "An extremely small earthquake. Indeed, possibly the smallest earthquake that has ever been noted. So small that it can scarcely be described as such."

"Enough!" King Zoser pants. "I can bear no more sophistry! It is enough that the infernal rodent is no more. Now perhaps we can return to the more comforting business of living each day as if it is no different from any other nor ever will be."

"That would be nice." Sinuhe is more hopeful than enthusiastic.

"And yet?" King Zoser knows better than to expect a neat conclusion to a sequence of events that has shaken him to his very marrow. It is true enough: if he were not one of them himself, he might almost suspect that the gods were playing a cruel joke. "You wish to make your report?"

"Exactly, your majesty." Sinuhe stands and adopts a thespian pose. He has always been fond of making reports, King Zoser recalls. His true vocation was that of actor rather than soldier but the Acting Academy wouldn't take him because of his withered arm and rheumy eye.

"Well?" King Zoser frowns away the introductory theatrics.

"There was a long and fierce battle," Sinuhe begins. "A battle the like of which I have never witnessed before. We sent men in their hundreds against the giant shrew, but the beast was voracious. Its side was as tough as copper and our spears were blunted as they struck. While we charged, the old woman who called herself 'Sybil' stayed within the shrew's belly and harangued us through a strange arrangement of tubes and cones that made her voice as loud as thunder. The shrew opened and closed its mouth and many of our soldiers were devoured."

"Hideous!" King Zoser wrinkles up his face. "But what did the old woman say? Did she offer apologies for her disruption of our sacred peace of mind? Did she offer compensation for the pillage of our granaries?"

Sinuhe shakes his head. "Not at all. She merely kept repeating her earlier story, as if she was attempting to justify her actions. She claimed again that she came from the future and that a mighty inventor named 'Daedalus' had both built the shrew and sent her back with it. She insisted the shrew was a 'time machine' and that her country, which she kept reminding us was called 'Greece', was in desperate need of food if it was to destroy the rival state of 'Troy'."

"Yes, yes! Is that all? I already know this..."

"Not all, lord. She also said that she could have travelled to any other time or place to steal grain for her people, but that we deserved to have our grain stolen because we were a very foolish people."

"What?" King Zoser clutches the arms of his throne. His knuckles turn the colour of camel's milk cheese. "The insolent virago! What was she implying by this?"

Sinuhe's voice drops an octave. "She continued by insulting you personally as a corrupt and ineffectual reactionary and criticising all of Egypt as a stagnant society. She said that we wasted massive resources on pointless tasks while neglecting to reform the living standards of our common people. She cited the pyramids as a prime example. I told her that I did not know what a 'pyramid' was but she laughed at me and called me a liar. It was our own fault that she had arrived in our time, she added, and we had no one to blame but ourselves."

"Outrageous!" King Zoser can barely speak for wrath. "There are no pyramids in Egypt, nor shall there ever be! I'll see to that!"

"She insisted that there would be many, very soon, and that it was you who had ordered them built in the first place! When the earthquake struck, and the shrew and herself hurtled down into the fissure, she called out that she would return in a century or two..."

King Zoser sighs. "Will the endless wheel ever revolve smoothly again? I fear that there is a crease in Mother Time's fabric that will never be ironed out. Go now, good Sinuhe, and leave me to ferment in my own despair. It's no use asking for justice in this world. The best we can hope for is mercy."

Sinuhe bows, retrieves his smashed helmet and departs in a flurry of needless gestures and devoted expressions.

"And that is in pitifully short supply..." King Zoser says to himself. But she is there to comfort him again, by his side, cool hands stroking his brow. "Ah, my little mausoleum, how pleased I am to have you here! But tell me, droplet of rain, what think you of this? The shrew came to punish us because we indulged in the building of pyramids, which have neither rhyme nor reason! Then it is Imhotep's fault, is it not?"

"It would seem so." His principal wife nods her slow, wise head. "Yes, that would seem logical enough, if a little harsh."

"What is to be done with him then? Tell me, my ibis in flight! Would it be going too far to extract his brains by way of his heels as Sobekneferure did to the nomadic insurgents in the ruins of Buto?"

"Too far. Banishment would be enough. To Nubia." Her eyes are glinting with a mysterious light all their own.

"Ah, my unarthritic bone, you are as considerate as ever!"

The bustle resumes once more. The shadow reappears, as if it were a stick waved in front of a candle that has been lit, extinguished and then lit again. It wavers, it teeters. Loaded down with charts and sundry pieces of papyrus, it staggers towards the throne.

"Imhotep!" King Zoser knits his fearsome brows.

"Here, your majesty!" Imhotep selects a drawing and offers it to the King. "I have done as you requested. Here is a great variety of designs for a mousetrap, none of which have anything to do with pyramids."

King Zoser studies the first drawing. "You lie! This is a pyramid!"

"Ah yes, possibly that one slipped through the net. Here, try this one…"

"It is also a pyramid!"

"A simple enough mistake, your majesty! Please be patient and take a look at this one. I know this will please you!"

"Yet another!" King Zoser rolls his eyes.

Imhotep breaks down. Tears spring out and cascade down his weathered cheeks. "Pyramids are all I do!" he wails.

They watch him cry for long minutes. Eventually, even hardened King Zoser is moved enough to offer the hapless architect a kind glance. Imhotep blows his nose in one of his designs and continues to sob.

"One last chance..." he blubbers.

King Zoser nods exasperated assent and Imhotep perks up almost instantly. With a great flourish, he hands King Zoser the largest piece of papyrus in his possession. The King takes it and squints. "What is it exactly?"

"A pyramid. Shall I order it built?"

"Over my dead body!"

"As you wish, my lord." Imhotep fumbles with the charts and trips in the long backwards retreat that any mortal must make in the presence of the god-king. One of his scrawls flutters away into the shadows, unseen by all save the one who sees all. She moves forward and picks it up, folding the crackling papyrus and concealing it within the folds of her garment.

King Zoser merely raises an eyebrow. He is too tired.

"A sketch for a most remarkable design." She smiles again and he feels himself once more ready to plough forward through this most ill-starred of days. "One of his best, I assure you."

"No, I have had enough of his infernal pyramids."

"This is not a pyramid, my lord. This is something quite different. A scarecrow. A scarecrow for a giant shrew. Despite your low opinion of his other work, this one will please you mightily, believe me."

The sigh is almost inaudible. "You have won me over again, dewdrop. Let me see it." King Zoser extends his hand.

"Not yet, my lord. You are tired. You must rest. In the morning, I will show you. There is still time."

"Time? I thought so too, once..."

"Cynicism, dear? Come now, let us sleep away our worries and deny such a day in our dreams." And she leads him by the hand from the throne and down private passageways to their bedroom. Her perfume curls like a finger whose purpose is to beckon and he stumbles forward in her wake. They find their bed, adorned with flowers and amethysts, and sweep all onto the floor and King Zoser yawns a mighty yawn and sits on the edge of the bed and stretches his arms, his crown falling down over one eye.

"I just need to clean my teeth. I won't be long." She is away from his arms as blithely as she had rushed into them. She is both the net and its caster, he decides as he repeats the yawn. There are no windows in this room but he can hear the swell of the river on the other side of the walls, for this bedroom is at ground level, which is as it should be. Only fools would ever sleep suspended in the air.

He toys with ideas as sleep digs its sharpened talons into the corners of his mind and lifts his damp brain out of his cranium, bearing it away with a laugh to the land of sweet oblivions. Some of these ideas are so startling that he knows he will have to share them with his wife on her return, even though he is too befuddled to understand either their source or their implications.

When she does return, he notices that her teeth are still black with the liquorice of late morning. Either her dental ablutions have been less than thorough or else she has lied to him.

"I have been thinking, my big piece of lapis lazuli, that things might be explained in one fell swoop."

"What things, my lord?"

"Oh, various discrepancies and suchlike." He removes his crown and places it on a little table by the side of the bed. "Such as how events have been moving too quickly for a single day. All that has unfolded since the sun rose, and was wrapped up before the sun fell again, should have taken place over the course of months. How did the messengers follow so closely on each other's heels? And how did Sinuhe arrive from Saqqara so rapidly? Something has been amiss. There are mysteries afoot and one solution occurs to me."

"Yes?" For once, his wife seems a little nervous.

"Let us suppose, for a moment, that everything the 'Sybil' said was true: that she was a visitor from another time and that her country was at war with another. What would happen if her rivals knew about her scheme to travel into the past to steal grain? Wouldn't they try to meddle in time travel themselves? Wouldn't they also seek to travel into the same past to thwart her machinations?"

"What an imagination you have!" His wife attempts a laugh, but it is hollow indeed. "And it is you who complain that things are too complex! Perhaps weariness has thrown a blanket over your senses?"

But King Zoser is warming to his theme. "If this 'Greece' had a time machine, why couldn't 'Troy' have one as well? Perhaps the skills of 'Daedalus' could be bought? Someone from this latter realm might have travelled back to a point before that of the 'Sybil', specifically to await her arrival. They could have used their own time travel powers to arrange matters so that everything came together on one single day, the arrival and destruction of the 'Sybil'. Time to such a person would be no more than the clay in the potter's hands."

"But wouldn't such a person stand out like a thumb struck by a copper hammer? Both in colour and rhythm of life? Wouldn't their very speech be different in their foreign mouths?"

"That depends on how well prepared they were before they arrived." King Zoser sighs. "Anyway, my beautiful rain cloud, I have had enough of such speculations. Let us lay our weary heads down and bolt the portals of consciousness. Come my arable acre, my fertile flood plain, my very own wonderful Helen." He frowns. "That's not an Egyptian name is it? Helen? Now that I come to think of it..."

She blushes slightly and hands him the piece of papyrus she had picked up from the floor on Imhotep's departure. "Take a look at this, my lord. Although I said that it would wait for the morning, I really do think that it will interest you."

King Zoser rubs his bleary eyes into an analogue of focus. "What is it?" He chews his lip. "A giant cat!" He shakes his head in weary wonderment. "And the ink is still wet! I don't understand..."

"A scarecrow. A scarecrow for a giant shrew." His wife takes the papyrus back and climbs into bed next to him. "It doesn't have to be built for a century or two yet. You may leave the construction work to your descendants."

"What is it called, this giant cat?"

"I had thought of naming it the 'Sphinx'. What do you think?"

King Zoser mumbles as he drifts off to sleep. "That will never catch on, my enigmatic oasis..."

And he dreams a series of strange dreams. And in the morning, and during all the days that follow, he begins to doubt that such a time ever really took place. All returns to normal. He listens to the reed pipes of musicians and follows the path of the palace spiders. He plays board games with his wife in the hollow gloom and watches the flooding of the Nile (stretched nerve in the body of the land, finger in the nostril of fecundity) and the bending of swords into sickles and back again. He calls for bread and beer and spits out the tiny grains that grind all teeth to dust. The year turns, forever turns, as it should.

But sometimes, when he ventures out upon the palace balconies, he seems to see anomalies in the distance. Far away, in the direction of Saqqara, he catches what appears to be an unnatural mirage, the rising up of what could almost be, did he not know better, the outlines of a pyramid, vast and unwonted and shimmering like a stone ghost.

At other times, at night, when he has called for too much beer, he is entertained by an illusion that makes him laugh and cry and clap his hands all at once. And though he knows it to be an illusion, it seems not so far removed from the general illusion that is life itself. Far away across the dunes, washed by the moon, a giant cat chases a giant mouse under the lolling tongue of the Dog Star.

The Universal Set

The stage represents a sparsely furnished attic room. It contains a bed, one chair and a table on which stands the model of an octahedron. There is a telescope on a tripod near the very large window. There is a spade that has been thrust into the floorboards and left there. The door opens and five men enter. They all have the same name. One of them is clearly the man who lives in this room. He strides forward with confidence but the others loiter in the vicinity of the door.

CARTER: Come in, come in! Don't be shy. And shut the door.

CARTER (closing it): It's just that I'm not used to being invited to a person's digs. I don't suppose any of us are. After a conference we normally go for a drink in a tavern. So this is your residence, is it? (He gazes around).

CARTER: Yes, it is. I like to keep it simple.

CARTER: I wish more things in life were simple. The train timetables in this town, for example. (He appeals to his colleagues for confirmation).

They nod. Then they disperse around the room. None of them sit on the chair or the bed. They pretend to be interested in the condition of the ceiling, in the walls. It's a slightly strained atmosphere. They don't know each other very well and in fact only met their host for the first time earlier that day.

CARTER: Come on, my friends. Relax! I didn't invite you up here for sinister reasons. I am an archaeologist like you. These are my digs.

Carter wanders over to the spade and touches it.

CARTER: I can see that! What were you digging for?

CARTER: My hunch is that there might be a tomb in a secret space between my floor and the ceiling of the room below. But I abandoned the task before any conclusive results were achieved. I was distracted by other matters. (Pause) What did you think of the conference? I am interested to hear your views.

CARTER: It was the Seventh Conclave of Carters, so naturally I expected something dramatic to mark the occasion. Many of the speakers were interesting and some of them were controversial. That's all I can say.

CARTER: What did you think of Carter's theory?

CARTER (frowning): Which one?

CARTER: The Carter who spoke after Carter but before Carter.

CARTER (carefully): He took an unusual angle.

CARTER: You don't have to be diplomatic here. My attic is high above the street and no one can hear us. (Pause) I think he babbled a lot of nonsense. Ancient Greeks and Trojans with time machines! What drivel.

CARTER: Less ridiculous than what that other Carter said about the urgent need for archaeologists to stop using the same name. You know the fellow I'm referring to. I thought that was unworthy of the conference. He just wanted to cause a stir and get his name talked about afterwards. It is an honour to be a Carter. What Carter would willingly give that up and revert to being called 'Gerald' or 'Malcolm' or 'Bunty' or whatever it was they were originally named? The audience laughed at him for that and he deserved it, frankly.

CARTER (arching an eyebrow): Frankly? My own name was Frank before I graduated and became a Carter. (Pause) Anyway, I brought you four fine fellows back here for a good reason. I didn't want to discuss it with you in a tavern or other public place. It's something that Carter said. It bothered me.

CARTER: What? You mean about the mummification of pickles?

CARTER: Not that Carter. The other Carter.

CARTER: The one who lectured on the gradient contrasts between Egypt and Aegypt? Rather an obscure subject, I thought.

CARTER: No, the other Carter. The Carter who went onto the podium after Carter. You know, the one with the tic in his left eye.

CARTER: Oh, *that* Carter. Yes, of course.

CARTER: Didn't his talk disturb you? It left me feeling worried.

CARTER (smiling): Pure speculation, that's all it was. Nothing to take seriously. You always get cranks at events of this kind. They provide light relief. He claimed that the latest advances in astronomy prove that the universe is shaped like a pyramid. We've always assumed it was a sphere or hypersphere, haven't we? He wants us to believe that the walls of reality slope to a point. An amusing conceit, nothing more. Harmless buffoonery. Why has it upset you so?

CARTER (softly): Because it has the ring of truth.

CARTER: The ring of truth? But that ring was lost millennia ago when Atlantis sank under the waves. How did he acquire it?

CARTER: Not that ring of truth. A different ring of truth. I am certain he is correct. The universe is shaped like a pyramid.

CARTER (rubbing his chin): What if it is?

CARTER: Don't you see? It changes everything we know about reality.

CARTER: In what way?

CARTER: Think about it. Use your mind. Use *logic*. That's what I always do. I apply logic to things. We must always be logical.

CARTER: You are right. (Pondering deeply) I am cogitating it right now. (Pause) Yes, I understand. I see what you are getting at. The ramifications are serious. But how may we confirm his claim? (He notices the telescope) You have a telescope! And it's night time. Why don't we try? I'll focus it on the furthest limits of the cosmos and then we can be sure. It will settle the question once and for all.

CARTER: The device is not powerful enough for that!

Carter ignores him, moves to the telescope, bends over it and peers down the wrong end. He swings it around on the tripod so it is pointing away from the window. Then he mutters for several moments, sighs deeply, stands slowly and rubs his eye. Finally he laughs and makes an exasperated gesture.

CARTER: Very curious. The universe looks like a distant room, like an attic room, just like this one but much smaller. That's a disappointment but at least I have proved it is not shaped like a pyramid. Carter was wrong! Maybe I should write an article about it and send it to an archaeology journal?

One of the other three Carters steps forward.

CARTER: I must confess that Carter's theory troubles me too.

CARTER: You as well? But what's there to worry about? I have just demonstrated that the universe is shaped like a room. How about those other two fellows over there. Do they share your unreasonable apprehension?

The two remaining Carters nod vigorously.

CARTER: I am amazed by your gullibility.

CARTER: They are not gullible. They are sensible. I'm not alone in worrying about a universe shaped like a pyramid. Out of the five of us gathered here, four share the same anxiety. That's a quorum, isn't it? A quorum of concern. Now let me tell you something. Many of us have hobbies that help us to relax. Mine is origami. I like to fold paper into interesting shapes. I mostly make shapes that are connected with my profession. I make the animals and gods of Egypt. Sometimes I replicate the puddings of Babylon or the elbows of Hittite kings. We all have hobbies, as I said. I was once friendly with a Carter who liked to try to toast bread on the fevered brows of malaria patients. He consistently failed but so what? It takes all kinds. But a few days ago I was playing with a piece of paper and suddenly...

*He is unable to continue. He wipes his
face with a cloth.*

CARTER: Oh, don't leave us in the lurch!

CARTER: Sorry. I find it difficult to face the facts.
My fingers worked on folding the paper and I
wasn't really thinking about what I was doing.
My original intention had been to make the god
Set, who I have made several times before, but
my fingers had other ideas and they ended up
creating…

CARTER: We are waiting. Keeping us in suspense
is unfair.

CARTER: The thing about Set is that he was the
most cunning and wicked of the gods. And what is
Set Theory? That's a topic for a future conference.
The linkages between the god Set and Set Theory.
I am always very logical. The Universal Set is the
Set of All Things and it includes the god Set and
Set Theory itself. But in our reality it's the actual
universe that is the Universal Set.

CARTER: You have wandered most decisively off
the point.

CARTER: I am sorry. What was I saying?

CARTER: What shape did you make with your origami skills?

CARTER (with great effort): An octahedron.

There is a long pause. The four other Carters first look at each other, then turn their frowns on Carter. They are disappointed by the revelation.

CARTER: Is that all? What's so special about that?

CARTER: Don't you know what an octahedron is? Don't you appreciate the truth about that particular shape? (He turns to gesture at the table) Can't you tell from looking at it? This is the very same model of an octahedron that I made for no good reason that fateful night. It stands there and mocks me.

CARTER: The model of an octahedron, you say?

CARTER: There's no disputing it.

CARTER: The *model?* But you can't have a model of an octahedron or indeed of any of the polyhedra. If you construct a model of one, you have constructed the thing itself. That isn't a model of an octahedron standing on the table. It's a genuine octahedron. I feel that I must point this out to you.

Carter (clutching his face in his hands): That makes it worse.

Carter (sympathetically): Sit down on the chair, old man, and tell me what ails you. I don't see why you are overreacting so strongly. Let's get to the bottom of the matter. You accidentally made an origami octahedron. Then what?

Carter (sobbing): Then I learned that the universe is shaped like a pyramid.

Carter: But I don't see the connection.

Carter: Take a closer look at that octahedron. What is the shape?

Carter: One of the regular polyhedra, of course. One of the five so-called Platonic solids. It has a regular and equal number of lines, angles and faces. It has eight faces, in fact, each one an equilateral triangle.

Carter: Exactly! In other words it resembles two pyramids joined base to base.

Carter: Yes, I suppose so. I hadn't thought of it like that.

Carter: People often think the simplest of the Platonic solids, the tetrahedron, is a type of pyramid, but it has a triangular base and has nothing to do with pyramids at all. But the octahedron is a different matter.

CARTER: Fair enough. But why does this matter?

CARTER: Think about it, man! Why would two pyramids join base to base? What is the only reasonable explanation for such behaviour?

CARTER (blushing a deep scarlet): Oh, yes I see.

CARTER: Don't be coy! Let me shout it aloud. They are mating. They are having sex. Two pyramids having intimate relations with each other. That's what an octahedron is and no one realised it before I did. How do you think that makes me feel? They are humping each other, that's the sordid truth!

CARTER (thoughtfully): Why is it sordid? It's surely only natural.

CARTER: Two pyramids. One male, one female. That's the most likely explanation for the situation. The result may be a third pyramid, a baby pyramid. There's always the risk of that. One of the pyramids will get itself pregnant.

CARTER: So? Another pyramid in the world. Is that a bad thing?

CARTER: Not before. But now, yes it is.

CARTER: Why? What has happened to change matters?

CARTER (biting his lip): The universe is also shaped like a pyramid. That's what! Now that we know pyramids have sex, that one might become a mother and give birth to a baby pyramid, our own situation becomes much more precarious. If the universe is a pyramid, doesn't that mean we are on the inside?

CARTER: Yes, but we have always been inside the universe.

CARTER: We are inside a pyramid-shaped universe now. That means we are inside a pyramid. And what is inside pyramids?

The Carters exchange looks.
They are dismayed.

CARTER (nervously): Mummies?

CARTER: Which means what? That we are...?

CARTER (reluctantly): Mummies.

CARTER (clapping his hands): Bingo! We are mummies, all of us. Everything else is a mummy too, everything that exists, because everything that exists does so inside the universe, and the universe is a pyramid.

CARTER: I am a mummy. I can't believe it. But I must believe it.

He turns to the other three Carters.
They are trembling.

CARTER: The Universal Set is a pyramid and we are members of that Set. We thought that Sets could be drawn like circles, but we were gravely mistaken. They have three dimensions. They are pyramids.

CARTER: I am a mummy. You are a mummy. Everything is a mummy! A sneeze is a mummy, a guitar is a mummy, an aardvark is a mummy too. A yeti is a mummy, a curry is a mummy, a tummy is a mummy, a daddy also! A ship is a mummy, a cloud is a mummy, a riptide is a mummy. Oh, woe! Woe is a mummy, for that matter. And matter is a mummy, all matter everywhere.

CARTER: We are going to have to accept it. We have no choice. But consider further. If pyramids have sex with other pyramids, which is something I've already proved, and if our universe is shaped like a pyramid, what does this imply? Doesn't it mean that our universe is capable of having sex too?

CARTER: With another universe...

CARTER: Absolutely! With another pyramid-shaped universe. In fact the act might be taking place already, just as it is with this octahedron here. And this also means there must be another bigger universe to contain the two mating universes. And if universes are pyramid-shaped, which does indeed seem to be the case, then that bigger universe must also be a pyramid, which means...

CARTER: That the Universal Set is a nasty piece of work. A rotter!

CARTER: Well, it also means we exist inside a pyramid that is inside another pyramid. What is inside pyramids? Mummies. Fine. But what happens when the pyramid itself is inside a pyramid? That smaller pyramid must be a mummy too. A pyramid that's a mummy! Let me say it again. A pyramid that's a mummy. Remain logical. Use logic, as I do. Let logic be your only guide.

CARTER: This is stupendous. This is atrocious.

CARTER: I am glad the full implications of what we are dealing with have percolated into your brain. A pyramid that's a mummy. The concept is staggering. We are inside the pyramid that is the universe, therefore we are mummies. But the universe is inside another pyramid. The universe is a mummy. Thus we are mummies of the mummy.

CARTER: That would make us grandmummies!

CARTER: You said it. We are grandmas, all of us, all of us in this room. We thought we were young and aspiring archaeologists. We thought we were going places. But in fact we are grans. Lovers of knitting and grumbling. Rocking chair squatters. Scarves and sweets advocates. You and you and you and you and me. Grannies. Listen to our old joints creak! Hearken to our poor worn bones. Let's shuffle off to the kitchen to put a kettle on the stove. When it whistles we can make a pot of tea. You are a granny, pal. Not a handsome fellow with a great career ahead of you. You're a gran, I'm a gran, we are all grans together. And that is logic!

CARTER: Quick! You must write all this in an article and submit it to a journal.

CARTER (Shaking his head sadly): My hand is quivering too much to hold a pen. It's just not possible for me to write anything at all. I am a gran and grans don't write. Do you understand?

Charlie don't surf and grans don't write. We are decrepit, crumbling, forgetful, set in our ways, arthritic.

CARTER: You are right! We are grans!

CARTER: We are doomed!

There is panic. The Carters rush around the room aimlessly, flapping their arms and shrieking. Two of them collide and rebound and resume rushing. Only the host Carter retains his dignity. He stands there, watching the proceedings. He is intrigued. One by one the Carters lose their frenzy and come to a standstill. Now four Carters wait for the host Carter to speak again.

CARTER: And yet, something doesn't seem quite right about it.

CARTER: In what manner?

CARTER: This isn't a manor. It's an attic in a normal house.

CARTER: In what way, is what I meant.

CARTER: I see. Well, it doesn't seem right that a quartet of grans would have adequate energy or flexibility to rush about aimlessly in the style that I have seen demonstrated just now. Could grans do that? Typical ones, never. Special ones, very rarely. And the chances of all four of you being special grans? Infinitesimally small. I now believe it is very unlikely we are grannies, after all.

CARTER: But is there an alternative explanation?

CARTER: There must be! (Pause) I believe we have been looking at it the wrong way round. Just as if we had been peering down the wrong end of a telescope. I think we have been putting the Carter before the Horus. We are simply too sprightly and lithe to be grans. Therefore we are not the mummies of a mummy.

CARTER: But you used logic to prove that we were!

CARTER: And now I am using logic to refute that proof. That's the greatest thing about logic. It is always capable of reversing direction. Let's think of it this way instead. We are in one universe. There is a bigger universe beyond it. The universe is our mother because it gave birth to us. This means the bigger universe is a mother of the mother. So we are not the grans. We are the children of the child.

CARTER: In other words, we are grandchildren?

CARTER: It must be! There's simply no other explanation. We are grandchildren. That is why you found it so easy to prance and caper just now. So much energy! So much flexibility! You flounced and gibbered. Oh, what a delight. But I fear this puts us in an even worse position than before.

CARTERS (all four together): How so?

CARTER: What happens to grandchildren? Think about it. What is the inevitable fate of such beings? What is *our* destiny now?

CARTER: I don't know.

CARTER: I have no idea.

CARTER: Please tell us!

CARTER (nodding slowly): Very well. Grandchildren get patted on the head. That is what happens, isn't it? Yes, it is.

CARTER (echoing): Patted on the head.

CARTER: And if we are grandchildren, which I now believe has been proved beyond a reasonable doubt, then the time for us to be patted on the head must be getting closer. It might happen tonight. Or even right now!

They all turn to look at the window.

CARTERS (in a whisper): Patted on the head...

A gigantic hand looms outside the window, palm downwards. It has obviously come to pat them on the head. The Carters jump back in alarm but remain transfixed by the sight. The hand moves closer, seeking to enter the attic room to discharge its duty but it finds the pane of glass in the way. The Carters gasp. The hand clenches itself into a fist as if preparing to punch through.

CARTER: Don't panic, my friends! Listen carefully to me. No hand could be that big. It would collapse under its own weight. Logic won't permit that hand to exist. The laws of physics and biology don't allow giants. That hand obviously belongs to a giant and giants don't exist. We are safe. (Pause) Unless...

CARTERS (screaming): Unless what?

CARTER: Unless that hand is a normal-sized hand. Just the hand of a normal human. If that's the case, then it means we are...

CARTERS: We are what?

CARTER: We are much smaller than we have always assumed. And that would mean we aren't real people but puppets! Logic! And that's only one hand, so where is the other? There are always two hands.

CARTERS: Where is the other one? What is it doing?

CARTER: What if it tries to surround us?

The other hand enters the stage from the wings. It is carrying a huge pair of scissors. Rapidly and skilfully it cuts the invisible strings of all the Carters. They tumble to the floor and remain there unmoving. The hand holding the scissors withdraws. The hand outside the window also is drawn back. There is a long pause. Then the octahedron on the table begins vibrating. It breaks apart into two pyramids. Slowly the lights are dimmed. The curtain closes.

A Tomb with a View

Carter said, "This is your tomb. It's coming along nicely. Mine will be right next to it. But yours has a better view."

Blunder nodded. "I'm pleased, but I don't want to openly display too much enthusiasm. Hence my reticence."

"Such manners! Obsolete, my friend."

"All the same, considering the gravity of the situation…"

Carter pounced on the word.

"Gravity! That's what it's all about, ultimately."

Blunder broke into a smile.

They stood at the base of the small hill and looked up to where the pyramid under construction stood. At this distance it seemed tiny, as indeed it really was, hardly taller than a man. It was two-thirds finished or more, and already a bright capstone stood adjacent to the structure, waiting to be hoisted into position. But the site was quiet now, the builders were resting. They would resume work later in the evening, when it was cooler.

Blunder asked, "Where is my viewing slit?"

"On the other side. You can't see it from here. It's on the side facing east and looking down to the Red Sea."

"Ah, that's nice." Blunder inhaled deeply.

Carter prodded a stone with the toe of his shoe. "For some reason, and I'll confess that I am surprised by this, people don't want to look at the sea. They're far more interested in having a view over the desert. The western slopes of Jabal Shaib al Banat are covered with tombs. That's not much of a view, to my way of thinking. I love watery horizons."

"Not much of a view in your view?" laughed Blunder.

Carter said, "Always witty."

But his face remained serious. He had no sense of humour. He straightened up and began climbing the hill on foot, beckoning to Blunder to follow. As they ascended, they panted like extinct leopards. Below, the battered chassis of their parked vehicle groaned and snapped as the metal expanded in the sun. Both men wore hats with very wide brims.

The hill was neither steep nor high, but they slipped often on loose stones. They reached the base of the pyramid twenty minutes later, gasping, crimson in the face, drenched in oily sweat.

"One week from now and you'll be able to occupy it," said Carter, fanning himself with his hat. He grinned.

This grin was one of paternal encouragement rather than mirth. He caught his breath fully while Blunder reached out to touch the stones. They were warm but not too hot. A porous mineral, self-cooling, but strong enough to withstand earthquakes. That was the thing about a pyramid shape. It was more stable than anything. It simply can't topple.

"I'm looking forward to moving in."

"Are you really?"

"Yes, because of the sea. It's a tomb with a view. We have to live in tombs, there's no choice, so it's best to accept what we can't change. All of us. That is the law and I won't oppose it."

"Wisdom comes with age. You are young."

"It comes *with* the age and what is the age? This is the age of men without souls. That's how it must be."

Carter enjoyed and admired the periodic stoicism of Blunder. It made his own role much easier. Blunder was now moving around the base of the edifice, shouting with satisfaction when he found the entrance and the observation slit. Then he reappeared, fingers still brushing the stone, his first circumnavigation of his final resting place. But how restful would it be in truth? He gazed at the distant sea, deceptively calm.

Carter was thinking along the same lines.

He sat down in the dust.

Blunder sat next to him. They were in the shade of the truncated pyramid. Carter chewed on a miswak stick.

"I am slightly worried, you know," he confessed. "Actually, you probably don't know. But I have been thinking, churning over and over in my mind the unhatched consequences of the situation we find ourselves in. I guess you've been doing the same and yet—"

"Oh, yes?" Blunder wasn't interested yet.

Carter removed the stick from his mouth, eyed it critically. His molars had frayed and splayed the blunt tip.

"Do you mind if I just verbalise a few of my ideas? It might help me. Just to relax a little. I mean, this is Egypt, the tombs belong here, they aren't out of place, but what about the rest of the world? How will pyramids look in London or Paris or Tokyo? Not that it matters. But the change was so sudden. Yes, I'm rambling. That's what I tend to do."

He paused but Blunder made no comment. Carter coughed. "Ghosts."

"That's right." Blunder nodded in approval.

Carter said, "Well, the concept of ghosts was one humanity had lived with for millennia. Some of us believed, some of us doubted. It didn't matter, did it? I remember a professor at university who was very sceptical. If ghosts exist and can pass through solid objects like walls with ease, then they don't interact at all with matter. That's physics. But they don't float off the surface of our world into space. This means what precisely? Ghosts are immaterial but subject to gravity. A very dangerous combination."

"That is how your professor lectured you?"

Carter nodded. "Yes."

"I never had professors like that," said Blunder. He removed his footwear, flexed his toes. "Gravity, huh?"

"Gravity. And what is the truth? Ghosts *do* exist. And they *are* subject to gravity. And they *can* pass through solid objects, in fact they have no choice in the matter. And the result is—"

"They are pulled down to the centre of the Earth. To the very core. That's where the gravity is strongest."

"If we didn't interact with matter, the same thing would happen to us, but it doesn't. It only happens to ghosts."

"To spirits, yes. Only to souls. Everybody knows this now, Carter. I fail to see the point you want to make."

Carter gestured at nothing in particular.

"Every time a man or woman dies, his or her soul is released, and that soul becomes a ghost, but it has no time to haunt anyone or anything because the pull of gravity tugs it down through the planetary crust into the scorching mantle and then further, all the way to the core, where it is instantly pressed into a massive sphere with all the other ghosts from history and prehistory that have preceded it. Every man and woman who has ever died, every animal too, and every plant. All crushed into a gargantuan orb."

Blunder rubbed his chin. "Right, there is a ball of spooks directly below us. For a long time we expected our own ghosts to join the eerie sphere when our time came. A new factor in the equation of existence. We would die and end up in that expanding soul bubble. We were horrified but accepting of the situation. Then there was an unexpected development. That's what these tombs are about, the pyramids. But we adapted."

Carter nodded, picked up a small stone, flicked it with idle force down the slope they had recently climbed.

"There's more. I *think* there's a lot more."

"Let me take over now."

Carter gave his assent with a small scowl.

Blunder said, "The development, the unexpected development. The sphere of ghosts got so large, accumulating so many spirits of the dead, that it started to exert an enormous phantasmic gravitational field of its own. Then it turned into an eschatological black hole."

"That's correct. A singularity."

"It began sucking *living* souls out of the bodies on the surface of the world. With a sudden slurp, the spirits of healthy individuals would detach themselves from the flesh and skeletons and nervous systems, and plunge down through all those layers of rock, solid and molten, to ultimately join the sphere, which grew denser as a consequence. The bodies on the surface continued to live. They no longer had souls but they lived."

"I think about that sphere and wonder how dense it is now. But what's the point? I'm not a mathematician."

"No, you're an archaeologist, a fearful one."

"Aren't you fearful too?"

"Of course I am. I don't mind admitting the fact. One day my soul is going to be sucked out of my body. And then I will be a zombie too. And exactly the same thing shall happen to you."

"Yes, to everyone. A world of zombies."

"What does that entail? We asked ourselves the question. What is the use of having a situation where zombies are aimlessly roaming the Earth? Better if they just stay in one place, in their tombs. Laws were passed. That's why these pyramids are being constructed."

"But there's more. There's something I dread."

Blunder licked his lips.

"Really? I want you to tell me. But first satisfy my mind on another issue. Why have some living souls already been sucked out but not all? Why do we still have *our* souls inside us?"

Carter replied, "Some souls are more tightly woven into living matter than others. That's all there is to it."

Blunder gazed at the pyramid again. "But it's lovely to have a tomb with a view, whatever else happens."

"Listen. This is what disturbs me. The sphere keeps growing denser and its gravity becomes stronger. Its *metaphysical* gravity. All the souls of all the living beings on the surface of the Earth will end up inside it, packed together. What if the gravity proves strong enough to snare souls from—" Carter paused, sobbed, hid his face, as if he was ashamed.

Blunder waited, benevolent and concerned.

Carter shuddered, controlled himself, continued in a weaker voice, "From other planets? From other solar systems? From other galaxies? What if the souls of some alien lifeforms, the living spirits of extraterrestrials, are dragged across the void to join the sphere?"

"Could its gravitational pull be that strong?"

"A cosmos of zombies."

"It's an abstract fear, sorry," responded Blunder, "and I don't intend to fret about it too much. Intergalactic monsters! Why should I worry about anything so unproven, so speculative?"

Very quietly, Carter answered, "But there's more. With the addition of the alien souls, the sphere will become even more powerful, unimaginably so. And its gravitational field will extend *beyond* the universe. The souls of the damned will be pulled out of Hell and compressed into that sphere. Hell is more distant than the furthest quasar. And then the souls inside the Devil and his demons. It might not even stop there. The souls in Heaven too, the souls of the angels, and even the supreme soul of the—"

"God almighty, I've had enough of this! It's lunatic rambling. You have no evidence of any kind whatsoever. I don't even *believe* in Hell and Heaven. It is sheer nonsense, whimsical gibberish. No black hole can be so forceful, whether it is real or phantasmagorical."

"Don't you understand? We will all be compressed in it together, mingling, our identities lost in an orb of horror. We simply don't know what those strange souls might be like. We don't—"

Once again Carter paused, this time because Blunder had staggered to his feet and was clutching his own body, his hands frantically exploring his chest, his throat, his stomach. His mouth was twisted, his eyes became dull. Blunder spoke in a curiously bleak tone.

"It's happening to me. It's happened. Sooner than I thought it would. You unnerved me with your talk. You triggered the event, the loss of my soul. The words, the ideas! I hated your nonsense. I lost my self-control and the knots of my soul came undone. It has gone."

"Is it descending now? I'm sorry, my friend."

"Yes, through the Earth."

"Thirty minutes or so before it reaches the core and is sucked right into the orb. Half an hour. I suggest you enter your tomb now. It isn't finished but I will wait with you for the workers."

"Will they accelerate the project?"

"With you inside the pyramid, I'm certain they will. And my own pyramid is next on the list. I will be your neighbour soon enough. Both of us zombies but keeping each other company."

"The view. I will always have that."

"That's the spirit!"

"No, no, it isn't. The spirit is down there, accelerating, hurtling towards the planet's core, and it will never have a view, never. It will just be smashed into a nightmare orb, an evil sphere, blended with all the souls of dead and living men and women and animals, vegetation too, and the dead and living souls of every future individual who might ever exist, ruthlessly compressed into the densest spectral object in the visible universe, isolated and yet smeared, waiting for the very first alien souls to turn up."

"So you believe me? Share my fears?"

"It will take them hundreds, thousands, millions of years to join us. That's a question of scale, the size of space. But they might be on their way already, a fleet of alien souls, an armada of demon ghosts, a host of things from between realities, impossible to imagine!"

Carter was unable to find sentiments to comfort his friend. Blunder didn't need them. He smiled an empty smile, his eyes glazed, his mouth slack, and he said coldly, the words coming from his mouth with the trace of an echo, as if he was a thoroughly hollow man:

"But my body has a nice tomb, a tomb with a view."

A
day
dawns
and the
dim horns
of the moon
fade to wisps
while the boats
that sail the sky
push out from sandy
forlorn shores with a
score of broken oarsmen
in every vessel desperate
to net those elusive clouds
huddled like evaporated dunes
on the shimmering cruel horizon
and bring them back to crush them
beneath giant stones and wring each
droplet of moisture from their bodies
to water the parched days of that other
egypt where the cumulus hunters palpitate

www.ingramcontent.com/pod-product-compliance
Lightning Source LLC
Chambersburg PA
CBHW030027200726
48283CB00012B/1390